From Pieces to Peace

From Pieces to Peace

A CHANCE TO BEGIN AGAIN
(REVISED EDITION)

Elaine P. Davis

Copyright © 2024 by Elaine P. Davis.

ISBN: Softcover   979-8-3694-3154-2
           eBook   979-8-3694-3155-9

All rights reserved. No part of this book may be reproduced or transmitted in any form or by any means, electronic or mechanical, including photocopying, recording, or by any information storage and retrieval system, without permission in writing from the copyright owner.

This is a work of fiction. Names, characters, places and incidents either are the product of the author's imagination or are used fictitiously, and any resemblance to any actual persons, living or dead, events, or locales is entirely coincidental.

Any people depicted in stock imagery provided by Getty Images are models, and such images are being used for illustrative purposes only. Certain stock imagery © Getty Images.

Print information available on the last page.

Rev. date: 11/11/2024

To order additional copies of this book, contact:
Xlibris
844-714-8691
www.Xlibris.com
Orders@Xlibris.com
862993

Table of Contents

One In A Million 1

Perfect Image 34

Illusions 66

A Life Wasted

There is nothing more sad;
accomplishing nothing, neither good nor bad.
Just floating along, never doing very much.
idling along doing this and such.
    A Life Wasted,
takes time to scream and shout.
    Life is Unfair,
and never figures it out.
From daily challenges that all others face,
    A Life Wasted
Never gets involved, or joins life's race.
    A Life Wasted,
Won't get up, when it gets knocked down,
Instead wallows in self-pity, while on the ground.
It never says, "Get up, I can try it again!"
But instead says…
"Why try? I can never win.
    A Life Wasted
It is sad this is true.
    A Life Wasted,
Don't let it be You!

Elaine P. Davis

One In A Million

Cynthia stood in her bathroom looking in the mirror. She was one very tired 35-year-old. It seemed as if it was just yesterday that she was prancing and dancing on the dance floor with her High School friends…without a care in this world.

But now twenty years later, a mother, a wife, and a career woman. She had it all. WooHoo?

She felt sick to her stomach, as if she needed to throw up. Downstairs she could hear Bryant making breakfast for their three-year-old son Terrence. She really did not think she could make it to Sunday service this morning; but did she have a choice, being the Pastor's wife carried its obligations and sitting up front and center giving out a righteous head nod and glorious amen every Sunday (*unless she had one foot in the grave) was expected.*

Where her heart really was, was in her soft comfortable bed, sleeping until tomorrow; when once again she would be back at work attending to the futures of teenagers; who could care less what the real world is like and in no hurry to find out. So why was she trying to get a PhD in Counseling? **INSANITY**, *at a higher level?*

"Cynthia! Cynthia! You need to hurry up it's almost time for us to leave." Bryant yelled from the kitchen. He loved to make breakfast for the family on Sunday morning. Making pancakes for his son bought him so much joy. Jennifer was now fifteen and had totally rejected his scrumptious pancake for a more figure flattering breakfast.

Jennifer frowned as she entered her mother usually immaculate kitchen.
"*Good morning, Daddy, what are you doing?*"
"*Good morning honey, what can I make you for breakfast.*"
"*No thanks, I think I'll just have juice.*"
"*Well suit yourself. Could you help your mother and get Terrence ready.?*"
Jennifer placed her little brother on her hip and started upstairs.
"*And Check on your mother.*"
Bryant found the remote and clicked on the local news. He was hoping to catch a clip of himself discussing his views on a new upcoming lottery game. There had been a lot of promotion, and Bryant had been an outspoken opposition voice against it.

"**Today** *we have Rev. Bryant Jackson with us to discuss his view on the New lottery game* "**Everyday Millionaire.**" *This game is expected to make more millionaires in the state of Georgia, than in any other state. Because unlike other games it appears to be more like a raffle. This game will name 7 one million-dollar winners every Monday night. But to kick it off this Monday night there will be just one, Every Day -Millionaire winner. Who will receive seven million dollars, for that week's total?* **plus** *a fifty-thousand dollars bonus when they make the claim.*

While many are very excited about this Rev. Bryant Jackson you have been a vocal opponent of this new gambling process."

"*Rev. Jackson, is there anything more you would like to say about this new game that is due to start this week? Has your position changed since this new referendum passed making this type of game possible?*"

"*Thank you for having me. This new game is another shameful attempt to raise revenue off the backs of the poor and disenfranchised. Especially when the state government refused to allocate the proceeds of this new "AGGRESSIVE" game to social programs, which would support those of our community that cannot find affordable housing, or Healthcare. It is the continued manner of reverse Robin Hood where you have the extremely poor supporting the extremely rich. The current proceeds pay for the education of the middle and upper middle-class students. While thousands, maybe millions cannot afford the bare necessities.*

Poor families will suffer even more. It is not good when people with little hope try to find it in a rigged system that is stacked against them. I would encourage the community to think before laying down their hard-earned money to play the lottery. I accept that the community voted for the lottery, and I respect the process. However, I wonder who will be there to pick up the pieces, the shattered lives that the lottery creates? I encourage my fellow Georgians Put your faith in God, not in a lottery ticket."

"*Thank you, Rev. Jackson, as always it is good to have your passionate views on this issue.*" *And this Monday night some lucky Georgian will be the* first, *Everyday Millionaire, worth 7 million dollars. This is Mark Springer Live from downtown Atlanta."*

Upstairs

Cynthia scanned a calendar on the back of the bathroom door when Jennifer **entered** with Terrence.

"Mom, are you okay? Dad said you should hurry up, it's about time to go. I'll get Terrence ready for you."

Cynthia replied, "Yes baby I'm okay and thanks."

As Jennifer turned to leave, she pivoted back to her mother. "Mama, Can I ask you something?"

"Sure, baby."

"Can I go to the mall with Mariah and Keshia after church today?"

"Baby, you know how your daddy feels about that sort of thing. If he says it's okay, it is okay with me."

Jennifer rolled her eyes. "Mommm, you know he will never let me go, couldn't you just talk to him for me?"

Cynthia sighed. "Alright, I will talk to him for you, but you still have to ask him."

Jennifer looked disappointed, with little hope or expectation.

Bryant came in after Jennifer, "Honey, you are not dressed, and it is almost time to go. Are you alright?"

"I'm just a little tired, and I'm moving a little slow this morning. Why don't you and Jennifer go on and I will be right behind you. I will be there before service starts."

"Well, okay I'll see you there. Are you sure you're, okay?"

"Yes, I'm fine." Bryant started to leave the room yelling for Jennifer, but before he leaves Cynthia petitioned her husband on behalf of her daughter.

"Bryant, Jennifer is going to ask you something and I want you to say yes."

"Yes? What's the question?"

"She is going to ask you to go to the mall with her friends after church."

"Cynthia, you know how I feel about young people walking around in a mall. It is a recipe for trouble."

Jen will soon be sixteen, she is a good girl, and we've done our job, at some point we've got to test the waters. She needs to know we trust her, okay."

Bryant gave a big sigh. "I'll think about it."

"No, trust our daughter. It is time to let go some. She will be going off to college soon. She needs some independence experiences."

"I'll see you at Church."

"Teach a Child as you…"

*"Please don't quote scripture to me…**Jennifer, Let's go**!"* Bryant said as he left Cynthia pondering what she would wear.

Cynthia pulled from her closet the expected attire for the Pastor's wife. It was a role she sometimes saw as a blessing and at times a curse. It was probably easier for her than others because she was brought up in this very church, so the congregation easily embraced her. But just like anything, **familiarity can bring discontent**.

Cynthia finished dressing, packed up Terrence and was on her way. As she passed through her kitchen, she was shocked, like every Sunday morning, *"How one man cooking one pancake, could wreck a kitchen."*

"Lord give me strength. Come on Terrence, we've got to make a stop."

On her way to church, Cynthia makes a stop at the CVS Drugstore to pick up a pregnancy test.

New Jerusalem Baptist Church

Rev. Jackson stood to dismiss the congregation while the choir sang Until We Gather Again.

"Before we leave today. I know that some of you will play the new lottery that starts tomorrow. I encourage you do not look to man to supply your needs but place your faith in God. He made us a promise and unlike the lottery, **"He's a sure thing**.*" May God bless and keep you, until we meet again."*

Bryant made his way to his office after passing through a gauntlet of well wishes, and requests for personal time.

Cynthia and the other women were in a group discussing upcoming church events; when a sassy, shapely, somewhat worldly dressed woman approached the group.

"Cookie! Your brother will be very happy to know that you are here. When did you get here?"

"Right after collection" flashing a mischievous smile.

"Ha, Ha, I am just kidding." They exchange cheek kisses

." How are you doing, you look tired."

"Oh, I'm okay." Said Cynthia.

"Are you sure you're, okay?"

"I'm fine, maybe just a little tired. What are you doing for dinner?"

"I thought I would spend some time with mom" Replied Cookie.

"Well Bryant has a meeting this afternoon, and Jennifer is going to the mall with her friends."

"WHAT?" You and Bryant are finally cutting the cord."*

"Well, we are trying."

"I know, we can meet tomorrow, it is a teacher's workday I really need to talk to you, we've not talked in a while."

"I know with all my jobs, hey, isn't that Michael. How is he since…?" Asked Cookie.

"He's doing okay; I think he tries to keep busy. You know it has only been a little over a year since Melissa's death. You know he did have a thing for you back in the day. Cynthia smiled.

"I don't remember." Cookie said with a sly smile'

"He's a good man, someone is going to snap him up."

"Well, they can just get to snapping, cause I'm not playing second fiddle to some **ghost**." Cookie smirked.

"**COOKIE!**" They both laughed.

Bryant's Office

KNOCK, KNOCK "Dad, can I come in?" Asked Jennifer.

"Of course, baby come in."

"Your sermon was very good today Daddy, not that they aren't always good."

"Thanks, and flattery will get you everything. How can I help you?"

"Well, Daddy I was wondering if I could go to the mall with Mariah and Keisha…we won't be long."

Bryant gave a long sigh. "Jennifer" He paused and took a big breath "**Guard your life, like your life depends on it.**" "In one minute, your life can be changed forever, one second, one wrong decision, can set your life on a completely different path. I love you so much; I don't want anything to ever happen to you."

"Daddy, I know you think I don't hear you, but I do. I value what you say to me more than you will ever know. I know you love me, and I would never do anything to make you shame of me."

Shame? Me? Baby, this is not about me." It is about the life that you choose to live, and taking your **own** path, and not the path that someone else may set for you." Then he gave his daughter a big smile and hug.

"Have a good time. Do you need any money?"

With a big smile, Jennifer said. "I'm a girl, we always need money."

"You are your mother's daughter for sure."

Metro Bimonthly Pastoral Conference

Bryant drove through the large iron gate of a community of mini mansions. Several prominent ministers lived in this celestial garden. One was a childhood friend, Reverand Joseph Barnes pastored the **House of Divine Grace** and boasted a membership well in the thousands. He was also the host for this bimonth's ministry meeting.

Bryant thought, the only reason he was probably in this association was because his father had been, for years, and NJBC was one of the oldest and respected black churches in the metro.

Bryant parked his 2011 Lexus next to Jags, BMW's Porsches, and every kind of luxury vehicle you can imagine. He rang the doorbell and was greeted by the maid in traditional dress. She led him to the library where the group was mingling and discussing various church concerns. These pastors were the cream of the crop in the metro area. Some had authored books, travelled to all parts of the world, even televised around the world.

"Bryant, come in, it's good to see you." Do you want to get something to eat before we get started?"

"No, I am fine."

Rev. Barnes called the group to order.

"Today agenda has one issue to be discussed. What will the message be concerning this new lottery?"

"Sister Hart?"

"I feel we should be giving the same message about the lottery."

"Rev. Hawkins?"

"We know they are going to play. So, what should we tell them about the church's portion of the winning? Is it a gift or should it be treated as tithes?"

"Rev. Ray, Do you have anything to say?"

"Well, we certainly, should encourage them to give from the total amount won, not the amount after taxes."

"Rev Johnson."

"I wonder do we have a right to expect anything. Or should we even accept the gift? Is this the devil's money?"

"Rev. Patterson?"

"I say leave it alone and let them be guided by the Lord. They may be led to give more than a tenth. But make sure they understand they should take nothing from the Lord."

"Rev Jackson? we know you have something to say."

Bryant took a deep breath, stood and button his jacket.

"Well, I can't tell any of you what to do. But I think everyone in here knows my stance on the lottery, and with that I say, "Good evening, to all of you until our next meeting."

As he was leaving the room Rev. Barnes said, "Excuse me for a moment while I walk Rev. Jackson to the door."

In the hall the two men paused.

"Jack, I know your feelings about this, but you know as well as I that they are going to play. You need to lighten up, this world is changing, and the church must be part of the change. We must serve our people where they are, if we are not there some of them will destroy themselves, along with what may be a blessing from God. **Lighten Up**!"

Bryant gave his childhood friend a long sad look and said.

"Thank you, Rev. Barnes, but the God I serve is the same yesterday, today and tomorrow… Good Afternoon.

At The Mall

Jennifer, Mariah, and Keisha stepped off the bus in front of Camp Creek Mall. This was the place to be on Sunday afternoon if you were a student at Central High School. Jennifer had only heard about the going on at the mall on Sunday. Who shaded who, who was talking to who; she never thought she would be right in the middle of the action all by herself?

Mariah and Jennifer had always been best friends, ever since she could remember Mariah had always been there. Even though she was a bit high maintenance. She was very self-assured and confident. Her honey brown skin and naturally curly light brown hair made her a force to be reckoned with at Central.

Keisha was more of a follower, who secretly wanted to be Mariah. She really did not know her own self-worth. She did not appreciate her own kind of beauty. But being friends with a girl like Mariah could make it very easy for someone to get lost in her brilliance.

But if the truth be told Mariah was a little jealous of Jennifer. Jennifer after all was the total package. She was beautiful and smart. Adults and students respected her. But what would you expect from the daughter of the pastor and the school counselor?

It was if she got a double dose of goodness, with a little extra sugar on top. **Her course in life was set.**

After walking around for a while, Mariah said, "Let's get some yogurt. I need to sit down my feet are killing me."

The girls took a table in the food court to enjoy their treat.

"I am so glad there is no school tomorrow." Said Keisha.

"Hey Jennifer, isn't that Divine, Girl who would name their child Divine?" Mariah said."

"A mother that thinks her baby is Divine, I know, I do." Jennifer smiled.

"Why don't you strut yourself over there and tell him your exact words? **"DIVINE, I know you must have come down from Heaven, because you are simply DIVINE!!!**

"Mariah and Keisha laughed teasing Jennifer about her lifelong crush.

"You think I won't? Watch me."

With that Jennifer took a deep breath, got up from the table and walked toward something she had dreamed of for so many years… to seduce her secret crush.

Standing in the Sport Store in his uniform was a tall slender young man completing a transaction. Jennifer pretended to look through the racks.

"Here is your change and thank you for shopping with us."

"Good afternoon, Miss, can I help you find something?"

"Well, it depends; if you got something for free up in this place, cause a sister ain't got no money." Jennifer smiled.

"Well, Ms. It just so happens we do."

"O… What?"

"Kind and friendly service."

Jennifer's heart melted at his sharp wit.

"Dee, where have you been? I haven't seen you at church lately, and I barely see you around school anymore."

"Well since mom passed, I've been trying to stay busy, helping dad out as much as possible. Plus, you know I will be going off to college next year and I need to make money."

"Mom thinks you will probably get a scholarship in basketball."

"I can't bank on that; after all I'm not exactly a star player. Anyway, I'm not so sure that I'm interested in sports that way, unless it is sports medicine. I'm interested in something for the long run. Ball scholarships are great, but they take up too much of your time. I want to enjoy my college experience."

"Well, I guess I better get back to the girls. It was good to see you and you need to get back to church the choir needs you and I miss you… standing behind me. Now give me a big hug, I can't go back over there to those two with nothing." They hugged and smiled.

Jennifer backed away singing *"Let's give them something to talk about."*

Teacher's Workday: Monday

Cynthia entered the Save Lo Grocery Store, where Cookie is at the Customer Care Counter. Cookie smiled at Cynthia, and mouthed, *"I will be with you in a minute."*

While waiting she remembered how close Cookie and she had been when they were young girls. She had been straight lace, and *"Cookie well she was a cookie."*

It had been just she and her mom, and she barely knew her father. Her mother had worked hard to give her a chance at life. And she was determined not to blow it; and so far, she was on track living the perfect middle class life.

Cookie on the other hand was always a wild child. She was the typical "preacher" kid, rebellious, defiant, and looking for any opportunity, anywhere to make trouble.

Cynthia often wondered how two kids brought up in the same house, with the same parents, could be so different.

Cookie and Bryant fire and ice relationship often made her feel like the rope in a tug of war.

Bryant saw Cookie as a self- centered air head, **Miss Pie in The Sky**. *She never finished anything and expected their parents to finance her crazy ideas. She was the red wine stain on their father's perfectly starched white Sunday shirt.*

Cookie saw Bryant as their father's lap puppy, whose whole existence was to please their father. He never pushed back on their father's wishes. He had planned Bryant's life from the cradle to the grave, and Bryant never questioned the blueprint.

Mr. Go-Along. *He hasn't an original thought in his head. Cookie would often say. Nevertheless, they both loved each other; but their view of each other limited the time they could spend together before a small war would breakout.*

And while Cynthia would never say it out loud; She sometimes wondered, was she and Bryant really the sellouts?

"Okay, I'm ready!" *the two locked arms and left for lunch, giggling just like when they were in high school.*

"Apple Bees is always crowded at lunchtime." Complained Cookie.

"Girl, I am so glad to see you, I really need to talk." Said Cynthia.

"What's wrong is Mr. **Good and Righteous** driving you nuts, Daddy's little boy, trying to run your life?

"Stop it. He is your brother, but he is my husband, and he's a good man…I think I'm pregnant." Whispered Cynthia.

"That's great, I'm going to be an auntie again."

"Great? I haven't taken the test yet; but I must tell you; I'm not happy about it. I am in the process of starting an advanced degree. This could mess everything up."

"Honey, I'm sorry but all I can tell you is it will work out in the end; it always does. Besides, you may be worrying about something that may not be, take the test, then you can weigh your options."

"*Options*, What options?" Cynthia gave a puzzled look.

Cookie sat back and gave a slight smile and raised eyebrow **"You Know."**

"You are crazy, your brother would have me burned like a harlot in the center of town."

Cookie gave out a mischievous laugh. "You know I was just kidding. I would never advise anyone to do that."

"I know, but I don't think I can handle this, I've got my perfect two. I'm finished.

"Well, let me tell you some good news. You know that I am the desk clerk over at the Westmont Hotel. I was at the desk singing and the supervisor Mr. Reagan heard me and referred me to the manager of the lounge.

So… I will be singing there on Thursday through Saturday starting this week. It is only three songs set at 9pm and 11pm, but this could be so good for my career. All sorts of people come in and out of Hotels. So, I was wondering if you and Bryant might see me opening night, this Thursday?"

"Cookie, I wish I could say yes, but you know your brother. I don't want to get your hopes up."

"I know he thinks I've thrown my life away because I didn't do it Daddy's way. But that just wasn't me, and he should accept me. How can we get where we need to be if he won't meet me halfway?"

"Honey, I'll do my best, but I won't promise, but I am very excited for you."

"Well, if he won't come, can't you?"

"Cookie, I don't know; it is different when you are married. He might see that as my going against him. Let me talk to him, maybe I can bring him around.

"Keep in mind you were my "Best Friend first." Cookie whined.

"Okay, enough with the drama." Cookie opened her pocketbook and pulled out two lottery slips"

"Give me a dollar."

Cynthia looking puzzled. "What?"

"Give me a dollar." Cookie demanded.

"What are you doing?"

"We're going to play this new lottery game. A Millionaire A Day." People are going nuts over this new game just think someone in Georgia is going to be a millionaire every day."

"Are you kidding me…didn't I just say a wife doesn't go against her husband. You know how he feels about the lottery."

"I see he is practicing daddy's tricks controlling people's thoughts, Girl take back your balls."

"Balls, first, I don't have Balls, and he doesn't control me."

"Oh yea, then why did you just give me his stance on the lottery…What's yours."

"Okay, give me that doggone ticket. How do you do this?"

"You pick six numbers."

"Okay, I'm 35, Bryant is thirty-seven, Jennifer is 15, Terrence is 3, I need 2 more numbers, we have been married for 17 years and we were married on May 5th."

Cynthia and Cookie returned to the store, Cookie printed and gave Cynthia her ticket as many customers looked amused with her purchase.

"Good Luck! The drawing is tonight."

"Yeah, right"

"Oh, and remember Thursday at 9 and 11"

Cynthia took a deep breath; "Cookie can I say something, I worry about you too. We are getting older, and let's face it, you do need to make preparation for old age. It is nice to pursue our dreams, but at some point, you must wake up and deal with reality. Bryant is the way he is because he loves you and he is concern about you, so don't be too hard on him."

"Sis, I deal with reality every day. Every day I have almost the same responsibilities that you do, I just choose to do it alone. Because I don't won't to wake up from my dreams right now. Give me a hug, I've got to get back to work. Call me with the results."

"Don't remind me."

Central High Counselor' Office

Cynthia was back at work when her desk phone rang.

"Hey Mom."

"Hey baby, you alright?"

Yes, I'm calling because Mariah and I thought we might go pick up some job applications at the mall. We saw some places advertising job openings.

"Mmmm, I don't know about that? Is your father home?"

"No, but mom, I could just pick up the application for experience kinda, career planning."
You know you didn't say much about your day at the mall yesterday."
"Oh, it was great. I saw Divine, he's working at the sport store."
"Will you be able to get Terrence by 4?"
"Oh sure, If I can't, I'll call."
"Be careful."
"I will, thanks mom."

Miss Shirley's Accessories

Jennifer was conversing with the manager about the application, Mariah was browsing the racks. She thanked the lady and prepared to leave.

"I am available on Saturday and on Sunday afternoon. I am very responsible; my biggest responsibility is picking up my little brother afterschool and keeping him until one of my parents come home."

"Well, I must say, I am impressed with you, so get your application back and we will go from there."

Jennifer smiled and turned toward Mariah.

Suddenly Mariah grabbed her and began pulling her out of the store, as they passed the threshold the bell began to ring.

"Hey, hey you come back here!
Come on run!" Mariah was dragging Jennifer from the store.
"No, I have no reason to run. Let's see what she wants."
Get back here, NOW!
"Yes mam, what's wrong?"
"Let me check your purse!" Jennifer handed the Lady her purse.
She pulled out a scarf.
"Come on, let's go."
"I don't know how that got in there."
"Sure, and you really wanted a job."

The phone rang in Cynthia's office.
"Hello, Cynthia Jackson, How may I help you?"
"Ms. Jackson, this is Angela, no one picked Terrence up. Is Jennifer coming for him today?"
"Uh, I'm sorry Angela I will be right there in a few minutes, I am sorry I have to go my cell phone is ringing. "It's Jennifer. Jennifer, are you OKAY?"

"Well yes and no, I need you to come to Miss Shirley's I will explain when you get here."
"I'm on my way."

"Good afternoon Ms. Jackson, I am so glad you are here."
"Thank you, where is my daughter?"
"Well, this store has a no tolerance policy on shoplifting. But you worked so well for my nephew to help him with his financial aid 2 years ago, that I wanted to help out."
"*Come with me, she is in my office.*" Jennifer and Mariah are sitting in opposite corners in the manager's office.

Cynthia embraced Jennifer, "Are you okay?"

Angrily, Jennifer asked, "Can we go?"

The store manager said, "Yes, I couldn't reach Mariah's parents, are you willing to contact her mother?

"Yes, I will. I will share the situation with her parents. Come on girls, let's go!"

"Thank you so much for your consideration. Said Cynthia.

"Ms. Jackson please talk to these girls; this is very serious. There won't be a second time."

Jennifer jumped into the back seat with Terrence, the car was silent. Mariah starts to say something, and Jennifer yelled,

"Just shut up!! Shut up?"

"Jennifer calm down. We will talk when we get home. Mariah just be quiet for now; we all need a cooling off time."

"Jennifer, stay with Terrence while I take Mariah in okay."

Cynthia walked Mariah to the door. "Ms. Jackson, Mom is not at home. She won't be in until later.

"Okay Mariah have Towanda call me tonight." "I will." Said Mariah.

The silence was deafening as Cynthia and Jennifer drove home. Jennifer went straight to her room. Cynthia started dinner and searched for the words she needed to say to her wounded daughter.

The phone rang and it was Bryant.

"Hi honey, You on your way home?"

"No, I wish but we got some issues here at the church. The HVAC has gone out and the repairman is talking crazy money to repair it, and I have to make a stop by Brother Richardson so I will be a little late. "How was your day?"

"Okay, I had lunch with Cookie, and she wants us to come hear her Thursday night at the hotel lounge."

"Mmm, You know how I feel about encouraging Cookie's nonsense."

"Well, think about it, she's family and needs our support too. You be careful, and I'll see when you get home and "I've got something to tell you when you get here."

"What?"

"It can wait. Love You."

Cynthia went into the bathroom and picked up the pregnancy test. Was she ready to deal with this...No.

Knock, Knock

Jennifer, Are you feeling better?"

"Yes mommy."

"Baby, what happened?"

"Mom, I am not sure. I went in for an application and the lady and I were talking, and Mariah was looking around. When we got ready to go, she started pulling me out of the store, saying come on let's get out of here. The alarm went off. The next thing I know, the lady is pulling a scarf out of my bag. Mom, why would Mariah do this to me? We are supposed to be best friends, like sisters. I never want to talk to her again."

"Well, honey, sometimes the people we love the most, will hurt us the worst. But before you end this relationship for life, take time to pray and meditate for guidance. Maybe this is an opportunity to help her. At least talk with her, after you have calmed down.... And remember what we always tell you **"Guard your life. Like your life depends on it. They both said it together."**

"Mom, for the first time I really understand what you and Daddy mean. If that lady had called the police. I would have a record, which would change my life forever."

"Is it alright if I don't come to dinner tonight, I think I'm going to bed early."

"That fine, I'll bring you up a sandwich later. Terrence is asleep, will you listen out for him for me?

"Sure, no problem."

Cynthia leaves as Jennifer looks at a picture of her and Mariah.

Bryant came through the door, "Honey, I'm sorry for being late, but; I got a call that Brother Richards was in the hospital. So, I decided to come home and check on him tomorrow. "What's for dinner?" I could eat a horse."

"Really, because what I am about to tell you will feel like horse meat going down."

"What?"

"I had to pick Jennifer and Mariah up from the mall today...for shoplifting."

"What?... What? was she doing at the mall TODAY?"

"I gave her permission to go she wanted to pick up a job application."

"JOB! Who said she could get a job?"

"She was doing it for experience."

"EXPERIENCE?"

"Would you please calm down and let me tell you what happened." Mariah put a scarf in Jennifer's purse, and the clerk called me and released them to me. I've talked to her, but she really needs fatherly and Godly counsel."

"Hold my dinner."

"I will. But check yourself before you talk to her. She is a good child. Don't break her spirit."

Bryant softly knocked on Jennifer's door. "Honey, can I come in?"

"Of course, daddy, come in."

"I hear you had a hard day, What happened?"

"I thought Mariah was my friend, but today I found out she really doesn't care about me at all. I thought of her as a sister…I can't believe she put that scarf in my bag. "She could have ruined my life. I can't believe it. What if that woman did not know Mom?" Jennifer's eyes filled with tears. "I never want to speak to her again."

"Honey, betrayal is nothing new in relationships. It happens all the time. But what we must do is forgive those that trespass against us. Keep in mind, forgiveness is not about the offender, it is about you…your spirit. It means you give it to God. And that releases you from revenge, so your heart can begin to heal. And God may have his perfect way with you. **Hate and distrust brews a bitter stew.**

"You were very fortunate this time. God was with you. Mariah did you a great wrong, but maybe you should pray for her healing too.

You are going to have to decide if this is a relationship, you're willing to lose, or worth fighting for. Pray about it."

"**Remember, Guard your life as if your life depends on it**." They said it in unison. I am not going to worry about you, you are such a good daughter.

I am so proud to call you, my child." He kissed her forehead and left Jennifer in her thoughts.

Cynthia listens as the phone rings until Mariah picks up.
"Hello, Ms. Jackson."
"Hi Mariah, may I speak to Towanda?"
"Well, she hasn't got home yet."
"What it's 7 O'clock. You are being truthful to me. Aren't you?"
"Yes Mam, she sometimes goes for drinks after work, or she may have gone over to her boyfriend's house. But as soon as she comes in, I promise I will tell her to call you."
"Okay, have you had something to eat?"
"Yes mam, I had something." *Mariah looked over at a popcorn bag.*
"Well Mariah, tell her to come by the school tomorrow around 3pm. Get some good rest tonight, Mariah, Be good."
"OK Ms. Jackson, I will.
Cynthia turned up the volume on the TV in the kitchen and continued with dinner
"And now here are the first numbers for the first EVERYDAY Millionaire the game that will make a Georgian a millionaire every day. And they are 17, 35, 37, 3, 5, and 15. These are the numbers picked by the state's first Everyday Millionaire. There is also a Bonus of 50,000 dollars for this person when they come forward. Congratulations!!!!!

"**O HELL**, *Cynthia covered her mouth with both her hands, as she stared at those numbers.* "Cookie as soon as you get this message "**CALL ME!**"

Tuesday Morning

"Well, Michael I guess we should call a meeting of the church council to discuss how to address the heating and air system. We must find it within our budget. These things happen." Said Bryant.
$20,000.00. It's a good thing we did not start on the fellowship hall project. I guess we will continue to stand a little closer together when we fellowship." Both men laughed.
So, Michael, it has been some time since Melissa passed away. How are you doing?"
"Tell me about it, since Melissa died, I have had a hard time making ends meet, her hospital bills even with insurance are overwhelming. But I tell

you, my son has really manned up. He's offering to pay bills, helps around the house, Melissa did a good job, she would be proud of him.

"Well, all of that is great but I wasn't talking about finance or house chores...How are you doing? You are still a young man. Said Bryant.

"I know, but I'm afraid... not that Melissa was perfect, and you know we kinda had to get married. She was a wonderful mother and wife. But we had a certain kind of love, and frankly, I am not sure if I want that kind of love again."

"I don't understand, what kind of love did you and she have? Asked Bryant.

"I held her in the highest respect. We had a solid marriage. She was a good woman, and she made me a better man. But I want to know passion...fire. I want someone like your sister. A challenge, she's like a box of chocolate cherries; All hard on the outside and overflowing with sweetness and excitement on the inside." He chuckled.

"MAN, you still carrying that old torch?" Bryant said shaking his head in disbelief.

"Hey, it never went out." And it would have happened if your daddy had not got in the way."

"And now that I have a daughter, I understand daddy." Bryant chuckled.

"Cookie is such a dreamer; she's my sister and I love her...but I'm not sure there is room enough in her dream for someone else.

She is singing over at the Westmont Hotel Thursday night. Cynthia wants to go see her. I don't want to encourage her foolishness. Anyway, Pray! Be careful what you ask for...you might get it.

Tuesday Afternoon

"Cookie this is the third message that I have left you. It is urgent that I speak with you."

Knock, Knock, Towanda, come in I'm glad you were able to make it. Please close the door."

"Did Mariah tell you the details about the Mall incident?"

"Yes, she did, and I am so sorry. Is Jennifer alright?"

"Yes, she is fine."

"Please tell her that Mariah is on shut down for a very long time."

"Towanda, I think Mariah is trying to get your attention. You need to find out what this is about. I think she may be spending too much time alone."

"Look Cyn, Towanda leaned forward with clinched teeth "I appreciate you getting the girls out of this mess, but don't tell me how to raise my daughter.

I work my ass to the bone to make sure Mariah has the very best. I don't need you, a school counselor with your perfect little life chastising me because I take a few moments for myself. So, again Thank You and have a nice evening." Towanda gave Cynthia a vein chilling stare as she closed the door firmly behind her.

"Well, that didn't go so well, I think I am going home." Just then the phone rang.

"**Cookie, it is about time you called get over here, I need to talk to you.**"

"What's going on?"

"I can't talk about it on the phone, can you come over here?"

"I could stop by the house this afternoon on my way home."

"No, Uh The McDonald's on Riverside at 4pm."

"OK"

"Wow this place is really in need of an update." Said Cookie as she sat down in the booth.

"I didn't ask you over here to critique the décor. Look at this!"

"What?" Cynthia placed the ticket on the table.

"Cookie did you hear the numbers for the lottery last night?"

"No, what?"

"This is the winning ticket for the new game. I am the first Georgia Millionaire, the wife of the big mouth preacher that protested the loudest. What am I going to do?"

"Wow call me crazy, but I don't see the problem. Can I have a new car? I promise I will pay you back."

"You are missing the point. I can't claim this money."

"Why not?"

"Bryant will be the laughingstock of the state. This is the biggest betrayal that I could ever do to him. He will not be able to hold his head up ever again."

Cookie laughed, "He'll get over it once you tell him "**We're rich!**"

"Shhh...I was thinking ...that you could claim the money for me."

"You think the sister of the big mouth preacher is any better? Besides, I am not so sure you could trust me, and I don't want to find out. Sorry Sis, I can't take that chance. I would love to be there to see his face." She snickered.

"Did You ask him about Thursday night?"

"COOKIE! Focus, we are talking about my problem, he's going to skin me alive."

"I don't know how to help you... because I don't see the problem, pick up the money and tell them you want to remain anonymous."

"There is a $50,000.00 bonus if you pick up publicly, while seven million dollars sound like a lot of money, fifty thousand is not something I can just thumb my nose at. That could help so many."

Cynthia raised her eyebrows and tried to look pitiful, begging Cookie for help.

"Please help me."

"No, No, I don't want to get involved. Sis you've got to grow a pair and tell your husband he's **RICH!**"

"Shhh, Now you don't want to get involved, I wish you had not tricked me into buying this ticket." Cynthia stood up to leave.

"Hey, are you coming Thursday night, aren't you?"

"It depends!" she said coldly.

"On what?"

"If I grow a pair!"

"Cynthia, don't leave like this." Cookie grabbed her hand.

"Bryant and I may not agree on much, but we both love you." Cynthia finally smiled and said, "I love you too."

"Just tell him. You will get through this. Cookie starts to sing…We've got some moneyyy and we are richhh.

School Library

Jennifer is sitting alone. Books are spread all over the table.

"Hey, Jennifer You look very lovely today."

Jennifer looked up and there was Divine standing looking down at her.

"Thanks, and what do you mean today? Don't I look good every day? She asked with a smile.

"Of course, what are you doing?"

"Trying to get some studying before mid-terms," Said Jennifer.

"Why you and your girl not sitting together?" They both glanced across the library where Mariah was sitting.

"We have a situation." Said Jennifer,

"Well, I don't know what it is about, but you two have been tight since sandbox days. Hope you can figure it out."

Jennifer looked at Mariah across the room.

"Thanks, I'm sure we will work it out, one way or the other.

Jackson's house

Bryant is in the bathroom, when he opens the cabinet, and the pregnancy test kit falls into the sink.
"What's this?" He heard Cynthia coming into the house downstairs. He placed the test back in the cabinet and headed to the kitchen.
"Hey, what's up?"
Looking guilty, Cynthia replied. "Nothing, what made you asked that?"
"Nothing, just making conversation."
"Bryant, we need to talk."
"Okay, well it's about family, and being supportive of family." Said Cynthia.
"Well, I've been known to be pro-family, kinda in the business, you know."
"Stop being a smart -ass Bryant."
"You seem a bit touchy, lately. Does this have something to do with what you want to talk about?
"I've not been touchy, maybe tired, but not touchy. It's about your sister."
"What has she done now?"
"Why do you assume it is something wrong, you know…she's right." You do have a self-righteous way of viewing people. Well, I hate to inform you Rev. Jackson you are not perfect. You mess up sometimes too." Cynthia headed upstairs to change.
Bryant looked at Terrence and said, "She was just like this when she was carrying you."
"What did you say, I can't talk to you. She stormed out of the room.
Upstairs she turned on the TV as she changed to prepare dinner.
"Mark, I am here at the store where the winning ticket was sold. This game is different because unlike other games the computer will pick the set of numbers that you have chosen. So, you are not hoping for the right combination of balls to pop up, but your own selected numbers.
The officials of the state lottery hope that the winner will be willing to accept an additional 50,000 dollars, by showing up to make their claim. Now here is my ticket for next Monday's when seven more Georgians will become millionaires.
and as you can see it tells the exact time and store number of where the ticket was sold. Which brings me to why I am at store #641 at 12:59 the winning ticket was sold at this store yesterday. So, look at this tape, we have masked her face, but if you think you know this person call her and let her know she is Georgia's first EveryDay Millionaire. This is Mark Jones WBTV channel 7.

Cynthia was frozen with her mouth open…**"O My God, Help Me, Jesus, O MY God, Help me Jesus. What am I going to do?"**

She heard Bryant turn on the TV downstairs. She rushed down the stairs near naked.

"What are you doing?" She stood there breathing heavily, she knew he always *watched the news at this time each day.* Bryant curiously replied. "Watching the news?"

"Well, I thought we would talk in the kitchen." We can finish our talk."

"Okay." Bryant got up and headed for the kitchen. When suddenly the phone rang, Bryant picked up the phone.

"Hello."

"Hello, Mr. Jackson, how are you, and your lovely wife?"

"Just fine and how can I help you?"

"Mr. Jackson, my name is Jeffrey Blass, of Blass Mercedes and Automotive Care. Mr. Jackson, if you look out your window, you will see a brand-new Mercedes parked in your driveway. We would like you to drive it and let us know if you like it. You are under no obligation, just drive it. Mr. Cook will be happy to answer any questions you may have."

"Mr. Blass, no offense, "Are you nuts? I have no need for a car like that Thank you."

Bryant looked out the window and sure enough there sat a man in a new car. Bryant waved good-bye to him and looked confused. "What in the world was that about?"

"There was a man in a brand-new MB in the yard and the man on the phone said it was for me."

"Maybe, it is some new type of promotion." Cynthia replied. The phone rang again. "Don't answer it, let this be family time."

Cynthia hurried to the kitchen to unplug the base phone.

"Hey, I'm home." Jennifer comes into the kitchen. She kissed both her parents on the cheeks.

"How was your day?"

"Okay, I guess. I saw Divine again today at the library."

"Hey that name keeps coming up. What's up?"

"Nothing Daddy, he's just different than the other boys. He dresses different, he walks different, and he talks different. He is just different in a good way."

"He is a nice boy, and he seems even more focus since his mother's death. He works and keeps up his studies too. She would be so proud of him." Said Cynthia.

"I know his father said he is helping out at home and saving for college too. He wants to be a doctor."

"That's a lot of money." Cynthia said. But he is smart, he will get financial aid, he will make it."

"Well, I've got more homework, said Jennifer. She headed for her room.

"Now my dear, I'm all ears. Just what is on your mind?"

"Well, there is a couple of things. First, it's about your sister."

"She hasn't done anything. She is singing at the hotel where she works on Thursday, and she wants us to come."

"And why would I do that? Cookie needs to grow up and stop living in La La Land...I can't encourage that nonsense."

"Nonsense?" Why is it nonsense that she is living her dream? Maybe she feels it is the gift God gave her." "Why is her gift any less than yours? I think you need to think about this...Anyway, I'm going. I've already asked mom to keep the kids. Cookie is family; she needs support and compassion just like all the other people we give it to. For once I understand how she feels."

Bryant looked at Cynthia curiously, **"Is there anything else you need to tell me?**

"No," Cynthia turned to the sink.

Bryant leaves the kitchen and goes back to the den to watch the evening news.

Jennifer's room
Jennifer' phone signals a text. It's Mariah.
"MEET ME TOMORROW, Our table."
Jennifer replied, **"No, I'm not ready yet."**
I miss you so much, please forgive me. Please talk to me, Lunch time our table.
Jennifer texted back**, "Later"**

Bryant notices that the phone is unplugged, and plugs it back in. As soon as he does it rings.

"Hello, Mr. Jackson, I was wondering if I could arrange an interview with you concerning the new Lottery game drawing?"

"Sir, for me it is a finished issue, it is legal, and I respect the process?"

"Obviously, you respect the process?" The voice said sarcastically.

"Pardon me? Bryant hung up the phone.

The phone rang again, and Bryant ignored the call and turned on the evening news.

The release of the store footage has sparked some controversy. Some have identified her as the wife of Rev. Jackson. And as you know was a big opponent of the lottery. We won't show her face for privacy reasons, but if you think you know her. Call her and let her

know we are waiting. This is Melinda Scott reporting live from the location where the state's first lottery ticket was sold. "Back to you Mark."

"CYNTHIA!" He ran upstairs.

"What the HELL have you done?"

"Bryant, calm down the children will hear you. Lower your voice."

Cynthia, that is you on that tape. YOU! The wife of the man that worked tirelessly to stop this frenzy, buying the first ticket. What were you thinking?"

Cynthia took a deep breath. "yes, it's me. I'm sorry. I made a big mistake; I was trying to tell you I didn't do it intentionally to hurt you. I never thought I would win, It just happened I'm so sorry, can you ever forgive me."

Bryant is breathing heavily, "I am so confused right now, How could this happen?"

"Cookie and I…"

"COOKIE! I should have known she was behind this. I warned you about hanging out with her."

With tight fists and through clinched teeth Bryant let out his frustration.

"I am so confused. I'm angry because my wife won the lottery " He chuckled.

"I am going to be the joke of the whole state, NO, The Biggest Hypocrite of the whole state. What were you thinking? I can't look at you right now. He walked out.

Thursday morning

Cynthia woke up in bed alone. She had not done this many mornings since their marriage 17 years ago, and especially not in anger like last night. "Lord, How do I make this RIGHT? She got up and pulled the test from the cabinet and closed the bathroom door.

Central High

Jennifer opened her locker, and a note fell out "Lunch 11:45 Your table. Divine. Jennifer smiled and folded the note.

Cynthia is in her office hiding. She was making a call when Divine knocked on her door.

"Good morning, Divine, It's good to see you, I have been hearing some really nice things about you lately."

"Really?"

"Jennifer is very impressed with you."

"I admire her too. She is a fine young lady."

"Thank you, how can I help you?" Cynthia asked.

"Well as you know, I will be a senior next year, and I want to start looking into financial aid for college."

"Good planning, I will put together some information for you." Said Cynthia.

"Thank you, Ms. Jackson. There is one other thing. "What's up with Jennifer and Mariah?"

"They have a conflict going on, but it will work itself out. Said Cynthia.

"Well, I hope so, because they look like sick puppies without each other. The one thing my mom told me before she passed away is that there is nothing more important than your relationships. She told me **"Always value your relationships.** *They are as precious as gold. She said when your relationship gets a little dull, you've got to shine them up. Maybe their relationship needs a little shining up."*

"That's nice, you know she is right. I will pass it on to Jen."

"Divine, I will get that aid package together for you, and something tells me your financial aid is going to be just fine." I've got to make some important calls. Thank you for coming by you will never know how much you have helped me. "Your mother was a good woman; we all miss her kind nature."

"Yes, she was, Thank you Mrs. Jackson."

New Jerusalem Baptist Church

Bryant was sitting in his office. He looked very defeated. He loved Cynthia as much as he loved to breathe. She had been his one and only true love. She had never disappointed him like this. She had always given him support. He simply was not equipped to handle a betrayal such as this. This was like a kick in the gut. Then there came a knock at his door.

"Come in…" The door opened and it was Divine.

"Well, long time, no see." Bryant rose to shake his hand.

"I know it has been a while, and I do miss not coming to church, but I am going to work it out, but until I do, don't worry, I haven't forgotten my teachings."

"What can I do for you?"

"I was looking for my dad. We are supposed to be going to get something to eat. We have to make an appointment to try to hold our family together these days."

"Son, your dad is very proud of you. He was saying that you really had his back since your mother left us."

"That's because I know he will always have mine. No matter what I do, it is good to know that I have someone who has my back, no matter what. The one thing I will always thank mom and dad for is teaching me that **Family is like Fabric. Tightly woven, and sometimes torn, but it can always be mended.**"

"Thanks Divine," Said Bryant.

"Just then Michael came in. "Hey Dee, you ready to go?"

Bryant stood up to embrace Divine. "You don't know how much you have helped me today."

"Déjà vu" said Divine.

"What?" asked Bryant.

"Oh nothing, good seeing you Rev. Jackson.

"You too."

11:45 Lunch table

Both girls arrived at their table on time. "You meeting Divine? Asked Jennifer.

"Yes, I think we have been conned. I didn't know your boyfriend had a nose problem." Said Mariah.

"He's not my boyfriend."

"Sure, why are you here?"

"No, the question is why are you here?" Said Mariah.

*"Because I was hoping I would see my best friend and I could ask her for forgiveness. The truth is I'm not sure why I did what I did. But I must admit that I might be jealous of your perfect life. Because mine is so raggedy. You are smart, pretty, and you have **two** parents that care about you."* Mariah was sincere.

"You really think my life is perfect? Girl there is no such thing. It is not easy being the daughter of a preacher and a teacher…PRESSURE… However, I do know that I am blessed. Mariah, I would be lying if I said I don't miss you, but it is going to take some time for me to feel safe around you." Jennifer said firmly.

Thursday night

Bryant walked into the kitchen and found a note on the table. He hurried upstairs and shortly after he ran back down. As he is going out the door, he is amazed by a long black limousine waiting in front of the house to pick him up.

Hotel Lounge

Cookie has just taken the stage, and Bryant is shown to a table up front. Bryant took a seat when suddenly, he got a tap on the shoulder. Cynthia was standing there looking beautiful. Bryant stood to salute her. "You look beautiful!"

"Thank you. I am so glad you came."

"Where are the kids?" Shhh…Tonight it's just you and me. Let's enjoy the show.

"Well, thank you for allowing me to spend some time with you tonight. I want to especially thank my brother and his beautiful wife, who was my best friend first for coming out to support me. Let me tell you family is so important, and I don't know what I would do without mine and all you. Because you see…"

"You're nobody, until somebody loves you, your nobody until somebody cares, you may possess the world and all its fortunes… but money can't keep you when you are growing old…"

Bryant and Cynthia toasted Cookie's success.

"Bryant, you know I love you; I would never do anything to disrespect you. Can you please forgive me? About the ticket, I never ever thought this would happen. But since it has can't we make the best of it"

"Cynthia, I want to apologize for my behavior last night. Please forgive me. I was so wrapped up in my own feelings. I am sorry for my selfishness."

They kissed and toasted the evening.

Friday Morning

Bryant was awoken by a knock at the door of the Presidential suite of the hotel. It was room service with breakfast and a note. Cynthia had already gone.

"Bryant, I've gone downstairs to accept the money. Mom and the children are with me. We will be back as soon as the conference is over.

Bryant quickly grabbed a slice of bacon from the cart and quickly got dressed.

Cynthia was receiving directions to what camera to speak to and her getting her make up. Bryant arrived and got the children and her mother up from their chairs and began positioning them behind her. He looked over and saw Cookie and retrieved her from the corner.
"Your family is waiting for you." Cookie smiled and took his hand.
Cynthia began to feel her nerves, "What should I say," she asked Bryant.
Speak from your heart, your family is behind you." He planted a kiss on her cheek.
"Good morning, my name is Cynthia Jackson, and I am Georgia's first EveryDay Millionaire. I don't know what else to say except my family and I are very grateful for this blessing, and we hope to be good stewards of this gift.
"What will you do with the money?"
Many of you are familiar with my husband Rev. Bryant Jackson. He still is a very opposed to legalized gambling." Another reporter yelled out another question.
"What will you say to your congregation on Sunday Rev. Jackson? Bryant took over the conference.
I will explain it in truth. We don't always understand God's ways, but I am sure his purpose will be made clear to us. We are family, and we stand united in our faith. I love my wife, the mother of my two children.
"Maybe three." Whispered Cynthia
"All I know that there may already have been **DIVINE** intervention."
Said Bryant. He looked out into the audience and saw Michael and Divine.
The Jackson's stayed in the hotel that weekend and celebrated with family and friends. They decided that the press would be unable to get to them inside the security of the hotel. But they both knew that things would be different once they returned to their **new normal life**.

Bryant asked his assistance pastor to cover the Sunday's service, but he knew the next Sunday would be upon him quickly. It would be the hardest day of his ministry since he spoke at his father's funeral.

Monday Morning Blues

Cynthia entered the teacher's lounge.

"Good morning" The looks were less than receptive. Everyone managed to give a dry cordial response. Finally, Elaine the biology teacher came by and said sarcastically.

"*Congratulations, and what are you doing here?*

"*What?*" Cynthia asked.

"*I work here! Wait a minute.*" She protested loudly. "*Is this, what this cool reception is about?*"

Just then the bell rang, and they all scattered like pigeons to their assigned holes; leaving Cynthia standing in the lounge, very confused, alone and rejected.

Cynthia started down the long hall to her office. She knew how the person felt when the police purposely walked him through a sea of reporters, when they had done a great injustice to society.

But her only crime was dumb luck... Why was everyone acting crazy over a few million dollars? Didn't they know she couldn't go home at 35 and eat chocolate cherries?

She could hear the whispers and feel the stares as she walked down the long hall to her office.

Suddenly, a voice on the PA system, a friendly voice of the school secretary, "Ms. Jackson, please come to the office, Ms. Jackson, please report to the office.

"Good morning Ms. James."

"Good morning, Ms. Jackson, the Principal would like to congratulate you and so would I." She came from her desk to embrace her. She was always kind and welcoming, but something told Cynthia she might have to hold her purse a little closer in the coming days.

"Thanks Ms. James."

Ms. Jacobs, the school principal, was standing in the doorway of her office. Cynthia had never been able to quiet feel her out. Their conversation was always awkward.

"*Come in Ms. Jackson, have a seat. This will not take long. First, congratulations, this must be an exciting time for you and your family. Which brings me to my concern? I am wondering;: What are your plans.?*"

"Excuse me, I don't understand?"

"*Well, Ms. Jackson, I have juniors and seniors that need their guidance counselor's full attention. Your leaving at this time of the year would be a big distraction for them, and the whole school.*"

"*Ms. Jacobs, I have no intention of resigning this school year. The thought never crossed my mind.*"

"*Well, I am glad to hear it. You are a smart lady...and I like that you put the student's first.*"

"Thank you!" She had never gotten a compliment before.

Cynthia got up to leave. "Ms. Jacobs, I haven't come up with an idea yet, but I would like to do something nice for the staff, if that is alright with you."

"Well, run it by me once you figure it out. And we will see how the administration feels about it. Have a good day or should I say another great day? She smiled slightly and went to her chair behind her very big desk."

Bryant was on the phone. *"No sir, I do not wish to be on your program. I have nothing to say, so if you please excuse me. I need to get my son to daycare."*

He hung up the phone and almost immediately it rang again.... Lord, give me strength. He started not to answer, but he saw it was Cynthia.

"Hi Honey."

"Hi, are you on your way to take Terrence to school?"

"I was thinking about keeping him with me today, and just hang out around here."

"Oh no, we agreed to keep our lives normal as possible until this blows over. Tomorrow is not going to make it any easier. You've done nothing wrong."

"I know you are right, let me go out and take my beating like a man."

"Honey, I'm sorry I put you in this situation, but we will get through it.

"Hey some would say *"If I had your hand, I would throw mine in."*

"Love You"

"Ditto"

Cynthia began checking her emails like she did every morning. She was astonished to see so many offers to sell or invitations to speak for foundation or asking for contributions and of course there were the haters. Money is surely an attention getter. Just then a knock came to her door. It was Elaine.

"Hey, come in. "You sure you want to be seen with a selfish, stupid, hypocrite?"

WHAT? said Elaine.

"Yes, that what some of the names they are calling me on my email." *People just don't know a few million dollars is nothing in this economy when you have two kids to feed and educate. But that's enough about my troubles, what brings you in."*

"Yeah, your troubles... Well, I need to schedule a time to finalize the college tour trip, and to talk about career day for next fall. But mostly, to give you a head's up on Mariah."

"Mariah? What is that little girl up to now?"

"Well, someone is accusing someone of being a homewrecker and a Ho, right now it is in twitter world, but it soon will be in our hallway. Especially, if Rachael Clark is involved. Since I don't have your troubles, I had better get to my class.

"Thanks for the inside information."

Westmont Hotel

Cookie was overwhelmed with the success of her opening weekend. She loved the applause, the lights, the glamour. It was everything she had hoped for and more.

"You were wonderful!" said Mr. Reagan as he approached the registration desk. "Everyone wants to know, Who, is the new lounge singer? People really liked you. You have brought life to the lounge."

"Thank you." Cookie said shyly.

"I am actually bringing in some of my friends for a night of good old school blues and jazz. I must tell you; he's connected. I can't wait for him to hear from you.

As Mr. Reagan left, Cookie could barely contain herself. Finally, it looked like she was getting her first real break. So many years; she had hoped for a chance... finally she would shut the mouths of everybody that didn't believe in her talent.

Bryant dropped off Terrence and went to see his friend, Pastor Barnes. It would be awkward after his self-righteous departure from the meeting last Sunday.

"Hello Brother Barnes"

"Hello Brother Jackson, and congratulations! How does it feel to be the richest hypocrite in the state of Georgia?" Barnes gave a big old belly laugh as he greeted his friend with a firm brotherly hug.

"Man, today the pastor needs a shepherd." Said Bryant.

"**Derrick,** Man, this thing is ripping me apart inside."

"In a few days I've got to stand in front of that congregation ... and I've got to say something. Frankly, I don't know ...what that is?"

Bryant shook his head as if he were in physical pain; but his pain was of the heart. He lifted his head, and Derrick could see the glassiness of his eyes.

"But that's the easy part. I LOVE CYNTHIA!" Bryant paused.

His eyes filled with tears, and his shoulders slumped. "**But I don't like her right now.** So, right now I'm faking it. The hard part is that in a million years, you could have never ever told me that she is just another **DECEITFUL, SELFISH** woman. I, I thought… **He labored to say the words**…I thought our love; our marriage was unbreakable."

Brother Barnes leaned back in his chair; "Bryant," He paused.

"I was sitting here listening to you and all I could think was, Am I sitting in the presence of God? Because all I could hear was **I this, I that**. You the natural man… the human man can do **nothing. Lean not on your own understanding**, but let the **Holy Spirit** have its perfect way.

This is just one tribulation. If she were sick, it would be easy. Because you would have everyone's support, but instead you have been humiliated by someone you love deeply. Knocked down a few pegs, your glass house shattered. What you have discovered is you and Cynthia are just like the rest of us. So, climb down from your high horse, because you got some work to do. **You must go to God, and he will direct your path.**"

Sunday Morning

Cynthia woke up and felt wet. She went to the bathroom and found she was not pregnant. Thank God she had dodged the bullet. Maybe it had been from all the stress on the job, home, school, just everything. But should she tell Bryant now? The fact that he thought she was pregnant might be why he had taken the situation so well. She decided to wait a few days before she would tell him.

*She also agreed not to spend any money until they had a chance to speak to a lawyer and do some proper financial planning. He was adamant that their lives should not change. She assumed it was the shock of the situation talking. She would give him a few more days with that too. Surely, he could not be serious… **Not spend any money.***

This Sunday morning was like any other Sunday, except this Sunday they were going into the lion's den as millionaires. They had no idea how they would be received. Cynthia took her regular seat; Jennifer was in the choir stand. Her mother and Bryant's mother were in place and Bryant was in the pulpit…Just like any other Sunday.

"*Good morning, My sisters and brothers* **of New Jerusalem Baptist Church.**"

Today, when you leave here, I want you to have a clear understanding of these three words.

Betrayal, Forgiveness, and Conviction

All of you are familiar with the saying **"With friends like these who needs enemies?**

Let me say that again **"With friends like these who needs enemies?"**

The definition of betrayal taken from Webster is **to deliver or expose to the enemy by treachery, unfaithful in guarding or fulfilling, disloyal; to seduce and then desert.**

In street terms we would say **to be two faced,** *or they talk out of both sides of the mouth. Saints you don't have to look very far in the Bible to find* **betrayal.**

It started with Adam and Eve to Paul in the new testament. Betrayal is nothing new to man, and it knows no boundaries. It happens between brothers and sisters, mothers and daughters, fathers and sons, and the list goes on and on. But understand this, there can only be betrayal if there **is a faithful loving, respectful, relationship in good standing…***You see you cannot be betrayed by someone you don't care about, because there is no expectation of trust. There must be a relationship in good standing of love of unquestioned loyalty.*

Betrayal **IS UNEXPECTED!** *Except in one case…Jesus knew Judas was shady. The betrayal was with the other eleven disciples. They could not believe this person, they had broken bread with, sat at their Lord's feet, slept among them, could have betrayed them… and their* **Beloved Lord. They thought of him as a brother.**

So, now as they sat in the upper room, I am sure they were **suspicious** *of each other, doubtful about their futures, filled with fear, realizing their human limitations. But then* **Jesus** *showed up. Once again to restore and reassure, that everything was going to be alright. And he bought a gift, a comforter. He brought with him the* **HOLY SPIRIT!** *"The HOLY SPIRT came too comfort them and sooth* **their hearts, souls, and their minds.** *And he does the same for us today.*

Now I want you to look at your own life. Have you ever been betrayed, by someone, or maybe you have betrayed someone you love…?

"What do you do?

After betrayal comes forgiveness just as Christ did on the cross, we must forgive those who trespass against us.

We are required to forgive our transgressor because it allows for our healing… It allows the human you to step aside…So that the **HOLY SPIRIT can RESTORE**…*Then*

You can stand on God's assurance, not man's (Hebrew 13:6) that we may be bold saying the Lord is my helper and I will not fear what man shall do unto me.

That we confess **our faults, our failures** *to one another and we will be* **Healed!**

"Ye' do I walk through the valley of the shallow of death. I will fear no evil for thou are with me. So, it is with CONVICTION that you are never alone. Man may forsake you but know that we can do all things through Christ Jesus. Amen.

Cynthia picked up Terrence and went directly to Bryant's office, **she was furious.** *Bryant came into the office. He could see that Cynthia was steaming. He removed his robe and hung it in the closet.*

"Are you alright?" Bryant asked.

"You tell me after that bus you just threw me under?"

"What are you talking about?"

Betrayal, how did I betray you? I made one bad DECISION! and you publicly stoned me. I guess now we are even."

"I don't understand, who said that message was directed at you?"

"I'll be in the car! And by the way, I'm not pregnant!"

The ride home was silent.

Perfect Image

The annual Christmas Office Party was festive as usual. However, everyone could feel the absence of Mr. Mac. He had suffered a massive heart attack in April and things had spun out of control for a moment; but Camille and Mrs. Mac had taken reign and righted the ship, and things were back on course.

The McMillan Corporation was not the largest business in the city; but it was respected. It included several franchise businesses, retail stores, and employed upwards of three hundred people. But its pride and joy was Perfect image Consultant Agency.

Perfect Image Consultant Firm was prized because it contracted with small and large companies in the city on how to image their companies in the community.

Mr. MacMillan was noted for his success. He was known for burning the candle at both ends and in the middle. But it had paid off. Perfect Image was his way of giving back to the community; by mentoring new businesses and encouraging large businesses to invest in the community.

Now with the expansion of the entertainment industry the potential for the agency was unlimited.

"Everyone can I have your attention? I know you are having a good time but I'm a party pooper. There is coffee and desserts coming out and I encourage all of you to have some before you leave, Archie will give you your keys after you blow into the breathalyzer before you leave. Everyone laughed...Just kidding."

"So, let's take this moment to reflect on this year's success despite the loss of our captain we stayed the course. Raise your glass and make one last toast to Mr. Mac. Without his hard work and vision none of us would be here.

I hope that everyone is happy with their bonus this year, make sure you save some for this year's SPRING FLING TEAM BUILDING cruise. Together we will make this company even greater.

Have a Merry Christmas! "Chloe will you and Archie pass out the presents?"

"We would love too. Said Chloe."

Chloe is dropped dead gorgeous and the face of Perfect Image.

She is the youngest daughter of James and Esther McMillan. She had been the apple of her father's eye. He often referred to her as the pretty one. From the crib he entered her into beauty pageants. Her crown and glory was when she placed second in the Miss Georgia Pageant. After that she began to fade. It was then that Mr. McMillan created the **Perfect Image Firm** and made her the face of the company.

She and Camille would go with her father when he would make presentations to companies on ways to improve their images and increase their profits margins. In a mostly man centered business few clients could resist her beauty and would sign up for some sort of plan, whether it be new employee uniforms or the location of the plant on the counter.

However, Chloe was getting older; and it was rumored that Camille was considering a new direction for the company. Chloe would not be needed since she did little or anything else except lend her face. Chloe had brought into the idea of the "Perfect Image."

She spared no expense to pamper herself every chance that she got. She was almost perfect to the naked eye, but she had her demons.

Esther MacMillan favored her oldest daughter, Camille. She considered Camille her "**Golden Child.**" Camille was a shrewd businesswoman, yet gentle and kind in her delivery. Camille was able to hold her own in any boardroom. She had a clear sense of logic, and an understanding of statistics; two valuable tools in the imaging game.

She could put together and conduct workshops for employees, locate resources to correct whatever problems a company might have; and make the tough decisions to get it done. She was her mother's golden girl.

But Camille's no non-sense manner also worked against her. She was 33 years old, and Mrs. McMillan was getting concerned about her daughter's future. She noticed that Camille was becoming a little too comfortable in her appearance. She often wore flats, and her clothes did not fit quite the way they should. She was using less and less make up and her hair, well…she was doing "The Natural thing." This wasn't a good look for a representative of an imaging firm, and now the CEO.

"Camille, come here, I want to talk to you." She walked her daughter over to the corner and handed her a gift. It was a thin box wrapped in Christmas paper. Camille unwrapped the package and opened the box. It was a six-month membership of a local gym.

"Well mom, are you doing daddy's bidding for him from the grave?"

Camille! I am surprised at the way you are receiving my gift, with such distrust I'm your mother." Smiled Esther.

"Mom, you are calling me fat."

"No, dear, but I am concerned about you, I am not calling you fat. You know, you are young, and you never focus on yourself anymore. It has been five years since Jonathan broke your heart. He's not worth your giving up on life. Haven't you ever heard that the sweetest revenge is living well?... I just want you to find your happiness again."

"Mom, I have moved on. What makes you think I have not?"

"Mmmm, Let's see...When was your last date? You never pamper yourself. Look at your nails, your hair, and **if I see that black suit one more time, I think I am going to scream.**"

"Well, why not give me a shopping spree...a gym membership? There is no way I'm going to some silly hookup gym."

"This is not all about you...Well it is. Your father died too young with heart disease, and I am concern about your health; but this is also a potential client. This gym is newly open. I want you to go undercover, and pick up on some of their weaknesses, so we can prepare a presentation for them. I'm thinking this gym could give LA Fitness a run for their money if marketed properly. Listen, I apologize if I offended you. But we mothers call it tough love... **I want grandchildren!**"

"**What about Chloe?** She can give you grandchildren. Said Camille.

Girl Please! If Chloe has children, I will end up raising them and her too, **NO Thanks!**"

Mrs. Mac hugged her daughter and left the party in her hands. "**Honey, see to it that everyone makes it home safe.**" She kissed her daughter's cheek, "**Merry Christmas.**"

Camille was in her office early. The holiday had been quite without her father. No one really felt like celebrating. Her mother had gone to Savannah to visit her sister. She and Chloe had met and had a cordial Christmas dinner. In a way she was glad to be back at work, when suddenly the phone rang.

"Good morning, Am I speaking to Camille McMillan?"

"Yes, this is Camille."

"Ms. McMillan, May I call you Camille?"

"Yes, I am comfortable with that, how can I help you?"

"My name is Elon Steele of the Women Business League. I am calling because you and two others have been nominated by the WBL for Women In Business Award."

Camille is speechless. "What does this mean?"

"It means you have impressed someone in the business community."

"You will receive a letter soon explaining the process, and if you have any questions, you can call me. The banquet is scheduled for June 21, can you put that date on your calendar. And of course, you will be hearing from us before that time for your photo shoot. Like I said you should receive your official letter today?"

"Can I get back to you, I am sure there are other women that are much more deserving than me." Said Camille.

"I see you are the jewel that was brought to our attention. We will need to schedule a time for an interview and photo shoot for an article in Woman's Business Magazine, **Congratulations! Stay wonderful."**

Camille hung up the phone slowly. This smelled like her mother's dirty work. But she would never admit it, so what is the point of confronting her? Camille looked across her desk and there was that darn membership certificate. No, she would not be manipulated by her mother or anyone else. She was happy with herself, and no one was going to control her.

Suddenly Chloe stormed into her office, and she was a bit warm. She walked pass Camille's assistant's desk and flung the door open.

"What's up Camille? All my credit cards have been cancelled except one and it is near the limit. I don't have time to play games with you."

"Calm down, Yes, I did cancel your cards. After looking at the past few months' statements, you are out of control. And I think it's time you have a more sophisticated image. Rather than running around like some eternal teenager. You will soon be thirty and if you don't change you are going to go from a young beauty to an old fool. If you haven't noticed all your pageant friends have grown up and moved on. I did it to get your attention.

"Wait a minute," Chloe laughed. "I know good and doggone well, you are not telling me I'm stuck in the past, you are the poster child for stuck in the past. You are fat, and all you do is lay on the couch and stuff your face. Because some good for nothing man stood you up at the alter 5 years ago. So, you tell me? "Who's the old fool?"

Chloe stormed out of the office.

Camille sat in her father's big boss chair and caught a glance of herself in her computer screen. She could see the double chin, bushy eyebrows, and dry skin. Her suit revealed the tomato bisque soup she had for lunch last week.

She pulled open the drawer to get a wet one to clean her lapel, and there they were her best friends Fritos, Cheetos, and Oreos. Usually, reserved for the afternoon, but after that blow up, she needed a few of her best friends to help get her through her day.

Camille was exhausted she had really put her nose to the grindstone the last few days, putting together a workshop for an upcoming client, along with Chloe's craziness and that nomination call, she was spent. She investigated her refrigerator to find something quick to eat. There wasn't much to choose from…there was two slices of pizza, and a few celery sticks and two chicken wings, this will do. After a quick shower, Camille found her way to the couch wearing her favorite night shirt, with her dinner in hand; she was ready to relax on her sofa and began her evening workout, Channel surfing on her 300-channel package, looking for some measure of entertainment.

"Ah shucks, she had just missed Law And Order. Maybe it was a marathon. No such luck… Next My Six Hundred Pound Life… That's it!... Camille dropped the pizza and got ready for bed.

December 31, 2:35 am
"Hello?"
"Camille, Camille, wake up"
"What? mom! Are you alright?"
"Yes, I'm fine. But your sister isn't."
Camille sat up in her bed. "What, is she alright?"
She's not hurt or anything, but Archie is on his way to pick you up to get her. She's at the East Lake Police Precinct."
"Why is she at the police station?"
"It's a long story, get up and get dress. Make sure to "wear a long coat, hat and shades.."
"What?"
"Camille, you don't want to be recognized at a Police station."
Archie soon arrived and following her mother's directions, Camille was dressed incognito. Archie laughed, "What's up Dick Tracey"
"Shut up I tell you I've had it playing nurse maid to Black Barbie I don't know when this child is going to grow up. Why is she at the police station and how did you get dragged into all this?"
"Well," **Archie explained,** *apparently, she was in the car with someone, and he got stopped. He had a warrant, and she didn't. So, they gave her a ride to the precinct. You know I can't say no to your mother, especially when it comes to her girls.*

Besides cheer up, look on the bright side, you get to spend New Year's Eve with me even if it is 4:00 in the morning."

Speaking of New Year's Eve, what are you doing tonight?"

"I will be rocking in the New Year's with the Peach drop." Said Camille. "What about you?"

"I will be at church, we have watch night service, then breakfast, and then home, would you like to come?' "I've invited Chloe. There is no better place to start the New Year off, than church."

"No, I don't like being out on New Year's Eve it's not safe, not even church. Do you remember the year that little boy was killed in the church?" said Camille.

"Well, if you change your mind, let me know.

"Archie? What do you know about this nomination thing? Is this some of mother's back room dealing?"

"Why are you asking me, I don't know." Said Archie.

"I just bet you don't. All I know is that I'm not happy having attention… that's Chloe's thing." Said Camille.

"I don't know …you have a lot to offer, you are beautiful, smart, and compassionated and it is time for you to come out of the shadows" said Archie.

"Ahh, you are too sweet…No, I am the ugly duckling…I know my place." Said Camille.

"But the ugly duckling became a beautiful swan." Said Archie.

New Year's Day

Chloe woke up that morning around 11:00. Camille was reading the paper. **"Well, you finally woke up, want some coffee?"**

Chloe stumbled toward the coffee pot and came to the table with a cup of piping hot coffee and sat next to her sister.

"I didn't say it last night, but thank you for picking me up… I had a chance to do some thinking while I was waiting for you to come. I understand what you were trying to say the other day in the office. My life is pathetic, I have not accomplished anything in my 29 years, and at this point I am scared that daddy may have taken my life to the grave with him. I was looking around in the club last night and everyone seemed so young. I don't belong there anymore. I don't belong at the business; I don't know where I belong.

Archie invited me to church tonight… I think I am going." I need something maybe I will find it there. Remember when we use to go to church every Sunday when we were little girls? I felt so special then. I want to feel that way again."

Camille reached over and touched her baby sister's hand.

"There is only one fool in this family and that's me. I had no right to close your cards without talking to you first. "That was the salt coming out in Sugar" "The Color Purple "the sisters' laughed. "And just like Sug, I guess I get a little jealous of you sometimes."

"Jealous of me? Whatever for? You're the one that has an MBA. You're the one who has been entrusted with the company, you are respected in the community, what am I… A Christmas ornament. I admire you. Even when Jonathan got that girl pregnant, and you had to call off your wedding, after everything had been planned…You were grace under fire.

Man, I would have punched everybody out. Jonathan, his mother, my mother, But you… you were calming everyone down, you even told him to go and do the right thing…Now that's class."

"Camille before that you were very active in the church. You were happy. We were. Do you think it is time for us to go back? Come and go to church with Archie and me tonight."

Camille took her sister's hand and pulled her close into a loving embrace *and said*

"I love you…maybe next year."

Esther was invited to a New Year Eve Party at the home of an old friend. She always made a stunning appearance, and although she was 56 years of age, she appeared much younger. It's true **"Black don't crack"**

She really needed to look her best tonight. It was the first real social gathering she had attended since **"Big Mac's** *death. He always liked it when she called him that. She knew that at some point she had to get it over with…"*
The pity looks, the I'm sorry, How are you doing? Blah, blah, blah.

The truth is Mac, and she had often talked about their departure. So, they made it a point to love each other every day. They promised that whoever was left behind would see every day as a celebration; because it would be one day closer to the day when they would once again be together. So, She took a deep breath and rang the doorbell.

December 31, 9:45 pm

Camille took a warm soothing bath, got her bottle of champagne, and sat it on the coffee table in front of the TV. She surfed for the best New Year's Eve celebration. "They really had not been that great since Dick Clark stopped hosting… and some of today's new artist… no talent…especially rap. Did they say Beyonce is going to perform? OKAY. Now we're talking. I'm ready for the New Year."

NJBC

Chloe walked into the church. The usher handed her a program and took a seat in the back. Archie saw her and motioned for her to come closer to the front. She got up and moved toward him. "Some of the people whispered welcome back, it's good to see you." It had been so long since she had been here, she was surprised that they still remembered her. After singing praise songs, the pastor stood and announced his sermon. "A CHANCE TO BEGIN AGAIN"

January 1, 1:10am
Camille awoke with her hair matted to her face and slobber on the couch. Everyone on the TV were laughing and hugging looking happy and singing. "WHAT?" She missed it. The New Year had come, and she had missed its arrival. She seems to miss out on everything life has to offer. Tears rolled down her chubby cheeks. "Will she always get left behind.

Esther made it through the party without any major breakdown as friends offered their support and recalled their dear friend. When the countdown began, she felt an emptiness; for 35 years Mac was there to kiss her at the stroke of midnight and say **Happy New Year, My Love**. But tonight, it would be friendly kisses on the cheek and encouraging embraces. Everyone had included her in the celebration; but her emotions had been stirred up by a voice; one she had not heard in years.

Maximum Impact is a very modern fitness center for both male and female clients. It is equipped with the most up to date fitness equipment, full size pool, individual rooms for massages, locker rooms, a sauna room, and childcare. Everything is shiny and brand new. Coming from the men's locker room and onto the main gym floor are four young men all registered trainers. This is obvious by their nearly perfectly sculptured bodies.

"Okay Fellows, It is January 2, and like every January 2nd here they come." Said Thomas.

Yeah, and by March they have all Marched right back to their soft comfy couches." Laughed Dino.

"Hey, stop bashing our clients you ought to hope that they come and stay. Remember they are the ones that pay the bills, and James you were not always Mr. Universe yourself." Said Sly.

"Yeah, thanks for reminding me."

Thomas continued his taunting of the incoming customers.

"Look at her, who does she think she's fooling? I can read her like a book. You can look at her and tell she is not serious about fitness. I can guarantee that her fine girlfriend got engaged Christmas and she doesn't want to be the fattest bridesmaid on the pictures. She will be out of here by the first of next month."

"O ye of little faith, I read her differently she looks like someone at a turning point. She is ready to pull off the old and begin a new life, she looks like someone who may have been hurt, and she's finally ready to let go, and start over."

"Well thank you Dr. Phil." I still say she will be out of here by next month."

"No way she is the kind that renews the same New York Resolution every year, by the time she is forty she will be weighing 200 + pounds. I would bet you she won't make it to February "Said James.

"That sounds like a bet I am willing to take a chance on," Said Dino.

"What?" Asked Sly. You guys are stupid. I'm not getting into that."

He walked onto the gym floor and directly to Camille.

"Good afternoon, welcome to **Maximum Impact**, how can I help you?"

"Well, I guess I am part of the New Year's Resolution crowd, but really I'M not. My mother gave me a gift certificate. Which is a smart promotional idea, I might add. I do have an important event coming up midyear."

"Let me guess a wedding?" Asked Sly.

"No, I don't do weddings." **Said Camille**. "But I have gone in a little deep with my weight and it is time for me to try to swim back to the shore."

"Well, let me show you around. We opened about 18 months ago, and I am proud to say that things are coming along. We offer the services of a personal trainer, of which I recommend it is an additional cost and we work with a Health nutritionist to help you understand how important food is in your health journey. So, are you ready to get started?"

"I'm ready! **Said Camille**. *Oh, usually people work around the trainer's schedule. I can't do that. I need the trainer to work around mine, and I like my privacy. I am willing to pay extra. No training with someone."*

"Okay. You are a lady that knows what she wants…and says it. I like that because I am that way too. We are going to get along just fine."

"Good, let's get you set up."

As Sly is pulling the paperwork together. Camille is looking around. She was now officially in undercover mode as well. There was not much to improve with the atmosphere of the place, so the weakness would be in the management. How would she find out how this place was being managed?

"So, have you been here since the beginning?"

"Yeah."

"Well, it must be a pretty good company to work for. I mean trainers are usually on the move."

"Yeah. It is a pretty good company and believe me I'm not going anywhere."

"Really? You could start your own business. I mean there are people out there that can't make it to the gym. Like me, I don't know how I am going to do this."

"You are going to do it, because I am officially a part of your team." Said Sly.

"I see you have a planner, let's get set up for the month."

He took a planner from his desk and Camille nearly passed out. She thought she was the only person left that still used a real notebook planner. They hashed out a fitness plan for the month of January and traded numbers. Camille gave him her personal cell number and she didn't want to reveal her undercover work at this time. She figured that he would be a good source of information about the operation of the company.

"Well, today is the first day of the rest of your new health journey. Ms. Ray, I look forward to our first session."

Camille used her mother's maiden name. She didn't want to reveal her identity right now.

Camille's office Jan 3,

Chloe came into Camille's office, "Hey, how did the gym go?"

"It was fine, I have a personal trainer," she said proudly.

"Good for you." Replied Chloe.

"The question is… are your 3 friends still in that desk drawer?"

"No, I evicted them yesterday. And I am meeting with the nutritionist this week to help with my diet."

"Well, maybe I will come and workout with you sometimes. My gym has become a serious hookup joint."

"Enough about me, What about you? How was church?" Asked Camille.

"Oh, Camille, it was like I had never left. Rev. Jackson remembered me, and he even asked about you and mom. The music was uplifting, and the members talk to you, not like when you are in the club, where people stand along the wall like vultures. I am so finished with that scene. But I've got to figure out what I am supposed to do. I know that my shelf life is reaching its expiration date."

Chloe paused. "So, I was wondering… maybe you could mentor me?"

"Mentor?" said Camille slowly. "Chloe, you've never shown an interest in this part of the business before. Why now?"

"I understand your hesitation, (pause) but like you said I am not a child anymore, it's time for me to put away my childish ways and become a productive member of this business. I finally accepted that we don't live forever. When daddy died, I guess I was in shock. Running around partying like a rock star, but I feel like God has given me another chance. I am willing to do whatever you need me to do." I think daddy would be proud that we are working so closely together."

Camille took a deep breath. "Give me a minute to absorb what you are saying. Right now, I have a lot on my plate, and adding on a mentee, at this time." Camille paused. "I just have to run it around in my head."

"I really appreciate your listening. Thanks." Chloe humbly leaves.

Camille was **raging** inside how dare her try to muscle onto her territory. All those years of her being paraded around like the pretty pony while she was the **work mule**. The years she spent sitting in the back of some run-down auditorium watching her tap and sing for some plastic crown or going to boring weekend events watching her dad argue with judges over her stage lighting or point value. She was right, all she had ever been just as she said; was a Christmas ornament good for nothing but show.

Now she wanted her to drag her along, while she plays catch up...

NO WAY! Just then the phone rang, it was Sly from the gym.

"Camille, I am looking forward to seeing you this afternoon."

"I'm so glad you called; I can't possibly make it today. I just had a little sit back and I'm just not in the frame of mind to work out today, can we reschedule?" There was a silence.

"Hell no."

"Excuse me?"

"I said, HELL NO! You are not going to waste my time with some bulls###, excuse like that, except for death of a family member I expect to see you here dressed and ready to go at our agreed upon time. (DIAL TONE)

What? He doesn't know who he is talking to...one thing she would be recommending is some sensitivity training for staff.

Esther's Office

Esther was in her office; she was putting in more time these days to help Camille keep things moving in the right direction. She had to admit that it felt good to be in power. She had not always agreed with Mac's direction with the business and their daughters.

She had chosen to yield, or it was easier to yield to him in major life decisions. He was a force to be reckoned with, and she just didn't have that kind of fight in her anymore. *You see Mac was just like her father, who was a man that would wrestle an alligator with one arm, and the devil with the other. I guess it is true that women marry their fathers.*

For example, he expected Camille to run the business, and never gave his beloved Chloe any expectations of substance. Those stupid pageants: what were they good for, *absolutely nothing.* However, she knew she was blessed to have a husband that loved her and their daughters so much.

"Ms. Mac, there is a Mr. Wilson on the line for you. Would you like for me to take a message?"

"No, I'll talk to him." Esther took a deep breath and straighten her hair, and picked up the phone, and in a professional voice... "Good afternoon, This is Esther MacMillan. How may I help you?"

"Esther, this is Wilson Carter." His voice held an old school excitement.

"O, Wilson, to what do I owe the pleasure?" She said coldly.

"You baby, my whole world has been turned upside down since New Year's Eve, I don't know if I am coming or going. You sure looked good to me!"

"Well...I see you are still shoveling it as well as you always did." She had to admit that his mischievous manner made her feel a little lightheaded. Just like she had when she was sixteen.

"No, no, no, I'm telling you the truth. You have upset my world all over again."

"How did you get my number?" Esther asked as if she was annoyed.

"Who doesn't know the MacMillan Corporation? Beside I've kept an eye on you through the years. I tried to get to you at the party, but you left right after I got there. But I saw you, and Girl you look **GOOD!** *Enough to Eat."*

"Wilson, I am not some Bimbo that you can talk all this thuggish nonsense to, that was why daddy was so against you. You still got street in you, what do you want?"

He laughed. *"Yeah, your old man did rain on our parade, but he never put out the flame that I carried for you.* **Please, please, please**, *have lunch with me. Just so I can hold your hand just one more time."*

"I am very busy these days, I don't have time." Said Esther.

"I promise if you have lunch with me, I will never bother you again. Let's just walk down memory lane one afternoon for old time sake." Please Esther.

Esther searched for the strength and common sense to turn him down and to deflate his enormous ego.

"Well alright, but let's meet at my house. I'll text you the address." What's your number?" She copied the number quickly. *"I really have to go."*

Esther hung up the phone and wondered. What in the **HELL** had she just done? She remembered that she was rarely in control when she was around Wilson. And where did those stupid words come from... *at my house?*

But she just did not want to be seen in public with him, not now. Wilson just did not present as the type of man that a woman like her should be seem with. Plus, she was still Mrs. Mac in the community's eyes. She had an image to protect. Yet, she could not help acting like that reckless teenager her father had fought so hard to protect her from this same ruthless wolf.

Feel the Burn...

Camille stormed into the gym with a huge chip on her shoulder, the nerve of a trainer, talking to her like that! She was good and ready to give him a piece of her mind; but intrigued to see how far he could push her. She had never had someone be so abrasive. It felt good to relinquish control to someone else. Was she sick?

"I'm glad you made it." He appeared to not appreciate her effort.

"Did I have a choice?" Smirked Camille.

"Yes, you always have a choice, and I'm glad you made the right one. I would have hated to terminate our relationship so soon."

"You are kidding? You would have terminated me for missing one session?"

"I see someone has not read the policy. "If a client misses the first scheduled trainer session or three consecutive session, that relationship is terminated. Reinstatement requires counseling and reassignment to a different trainer."

"Wow, that's a pretty harsh reaction. What's the rationale behind that?"

"The counseling is to deal with "Why" that person is not ready to change their life. What are they holding on to, that makes them afraid to take control of their life? The new trainer because the first one failed to inspire you to live your best life."

Enough talk....Let's get started.

Blossoming Love

Archie nervously dialed Chloe's number. *"Hey, what are you doing?"*

"Archie, what a pleasant surprise? Nothing much, what do you have in mind?" Asked Chloe.

*"Meet me at Apple Bees on Piedmont Road. We can do a **two for twenty**. That's about all I can afford."*

"Boy, What you are talking about? I love me some Apple Bees. See you in thirty." Chloe leaped into action.

"GOOD WORK! And you survived. Now, you are going to be a little sore. But that's good, go home, and take a warm shower and get plenty of sleep. Of course, you could get a massage. Our masseuse is here." Sly was strictly business.

Just as they were finishing; a shapely young woman walked by and for just a moment his eye followed her.

"Well, I see why they call you Sly."

"What?"

"I saw you checking her out!"

"No, I really was looking at her shoes, they caught my eye. And they call me Sly because I would cut you if you called me by my real name ... **Sylvester**. I don't know what my mother was thinking. He shook his head in disbelief.

"The only Sylvester I know is the cat, "I thought I saw a Tweetie bird." They both laughed. Someone had finally let their guard down.

"**Sly**, thank you for kicking me in the butt today on the phone. For the last few years people have let me take the easy way out. And my prescription has been **"flight over fight."** It's time I got back into the game of life. I really have some work to do. This company is lucky to have you."

"Well, thank you Ms. Ray, I am blessed to have you as a client." Said Sly.

"Let me ask you something has the company said anything about franchising **MI** Asked Camille.

"It's funny that you mentioned that. That came up at the last meeting." Said Sly.

"Really, how often do you meet?"

"We meet every Monday...my, my, you are a curious one. Are you interested in a franchise?"

"You never know." Camille raised her eyebrows.

"Archie, this was a great idea. I was about to take out a frozen dinner, this is so much better."

"Okay, I talked to Camille like you told me and she said she would get back to me. I must admit, I was nervous talking to her. I think she was shocked too. I did everything you told me to do."

"Well, that is the real reason I asked you here tonight. She talked to me this afternoon. She and your mother met, and guess who has a new assistance."

Chloe looked puzzled. "ME!" said Archie. "They want me to mentor you and bring you up to snuff of the business."

Chloe squealed with joy. "Thank you, I promise I will be the best student, like a sponge."

"I'm sure you will. I know you've always sold yourself short. You have a lot to offer, and I look forward to working with you."

They smiled warmly at each other. "Hey, I'm going to Bible study tonight, you want to come?" Said Archie.

They won't mind, sure?" Chloe smiled.

Behind Closed Doors

The doorbell rang and Esther could feel her heartbeat. She took a deep breath and opened the door. She was transformed into the teenage girl that burned with desire for this man over thirty years ago.

"Come in, welcome." Esther extended her hand. But Wilson was up to his old tricks. He grabbed her and pulled her close, tightly in a bear hug. Esther managed to wiggle out of his grasp and lead him to the dining room. For some odd reason she had made a great effort to make the table beautiful. This was the way she dreamed that every night would have been like if their love had been allowed to thrive.

"All of this for me? **Asked Wilson.** *Esther this was not necessary. You know I'm a brown paper bag kinda guy.*

"O have a seat; I will be right back."

She headed for the kitchen to collect the salads that she had prepared for lunch. As she closed the refrigerator door, and found Wilson was ready for dessert. She felt his arms wrapped tightly around her waist. He spun her around and their lips pressed firmly, and she was sixteen again.

Esther could not believe it. She was lying in the arms of the man she was not allowed to have so many years ago. It had been an exciting afternoon for a moment. But not one she was proud of; she was too old for this. She felt as if she had cheated on Mac; he had not been gone a year and she was already in bed with a man that had brought her only heartache so many years ago.

She was trying to think of a way to bring this train wreck to an end. Suddenly, she heard Wilson call out her name. She jumped from the bed and ran to the bathroom. There she found him, holding his chest doubled over in pain. "Take me to the hospital. I feel like I'm having a heart attack.

She helped him to her bed.

Esther ran to the phone and called Archie, get over here now. And do not bring Chloe! Then she called 911. She looked at the salad spilled all over the floor in the kitchen.

"Wilson, I've called 911, Is there anyone I need to call for you? He gruntled in pain, struggling for his breath. "Don't talk, just stay calm."

The ambulance was there in about 7 minutes, but it felt like forever. Wilson was experiencing a lot of pain. Once the technicians were in the house they began aiding him; blood pressure cuff, oxygen mask, and IV. They were asking questions that Esther could not answer. She felt stupid, saying repeatedly. "I don't know."

"Is he allergic to any medications?"

Has he had a heart attack before?" Have you taken any sexual enhancement medications?"

Wilson answered "Uh, uh..."

"Sir, it is very important that you tell us; so, we can properly treat you." Finally, he said it.

"Yes, Yes I took Viagra." Esther was embarrassed.

Ms. Mac Millan we are taking him to Piedmont Hospital, do you want to ride in the ambulance?

"No, I will follow." She took his hand. "Wilson is there anyone you want me to call?"

"Yes, I guess you should call my wife. She works at Costco on Westmont." Esther immediately let go of his hand. "What's her name?"

"Juanita, Juanita Carter." He said.

Just then Archie ran through the door. "Mrs. Mac, are you alright?"

"Yes, Archie I'm fine. Mr. Wilson got sick, and I had to call for help. They are taking him to Piedmont. I need you to call Costco on Westmont and contact Mrs. Juanita Carter. Let her know that her husband has been taken to Piedmont, and she needs to come quickly. Make sure she knows he is stable. Then come directly to the hospital and pick me up. I will be standing outside of the Emergency Room entrance. She then turned to the driver and said Are we ready to go?"

She climbed into the ambulance. It was the right thing to do. While on the way to the hospital she was thinking. How could she have been so stupid? She was not some schoolgirl unable to control her pussy. She was a mature woman with two grown daughters. What would they have thought of her?

It was bad enough that poor Archie had to be caught in the middle. He was like a son to her; she saw his face when he looked at the salad on the kitchen floor. What must he be thinking? She was so embarrassed.

She prayed that Wilson would be fine because if he died, she might have to talk to the police. This could get messy. Once she reached the hospital; she searched his wallet for a health card. She found his license, and there it was... his life...an old photo of him, his three kids, and his wife.

She gave the hospital his card and told them someone would be there soon to complete his documents. She walked out the emergency room door and into the sunlight.

She could see clearly now. This was a big mistake. The noise of the city reminded her that life can get a little crazy and confusing sometimes. But when we take a wrong turn, we must get off this street and get back on the right path. She thanked God for his grace and asked for his forgiveness.

Suddenly two ladies rushed pass her, one was Juanita. She could tell from the picture and the other a friend probably. She had made that same walk less than a year ago...She hoped Juanita would not have to travel the same path. While she was sure Wilson was probably far from the perfect husband; marriage relationships are complicated, and she was sure there was a loving relationship of some sort between them.

Wilson had not told her he was married, and she had not bothered to ask. She knew deep down that she had lured him there exactly for what happened. She could not play the victim here. In a way she had used Wilson to settle an old debt with her father.

He said Wilson was low class, and would have loaded her up with babies, and cheated on her every chance he got. She hated to admit it, but her father had been right. He was no longer the forbidden fruit. She had finally had a bite, and it left a bitter taste in her mouth.

Archie drove up, got out to open the passenger door for her; and never said a word about the situation. Once again, he was her white knight.

No pain, no gain

The first couple of weeks had gone well. Camille had lost a total of seven pounds, and she felt wonderful, both inside and out. She found she really liked Sly's style. He was very serious and professional. He reminded her of her father, or maybe she was just missing him. After all he had been the only man in her life since Jonathan.

Sly was very knowledgeable of his craft. He gave attention to detail and expected nothing but your best effort. He made her feel she was his most important client.

The one thing Sly had emphasized was she must prepare her meals, which meant she would have to cook. Which meant she would have to go to the grocery store. She had to admit this was not her comfort zone.

Normally, she ran in the grocery store for one or two items at a time. But she was trying to change her reclusive ways. Her list included coffee, one vice she would **never** give up. As she came down the aisle, out of the corner of her eye she caught a glimpse of Sly. He was with a young woman and a small child. They were reading the label on a can. Camille quickly got her coffee and headed for the cashier.

Driving home she was trying to identify the feelings that made her run out of the store like that. *Sly was her trainer,* of course he had a life outside of the gym. But he didn't say he did not have any children. She knew he was a bit older than she. She couldn't remember if it had come up. Now she wished she had paid better attention. Her brain seemed to turn into mush when she was with him.

Wait…Wait, calm down Breathe. Sly is just your trainer. Breathe.

Sweet Dreams…

Camille got ready for bed, and she was still going nuts. *Why had she reacted like she had in the store? Was she having feelings for her trainer? I guess it is normal for most women to have a crush on their trainer.* This emotional agony would probably go away. She just needed a good night's rest. She had a presentation the next day and was taking Chloe and Archie with her. This would be the first time they would have all gone out together as a team.

After working out that morning and working all day she was very tired. She was asleep before her head hit the pillow. But it was not a restful night sleep. She tossed and turned; she could feel the weight of a man on her chest. She struggled to break free, but he was pressing his lips against hers, forcing his tongue into her mouth. She could feel her body fighting…reluctant to give in to the heat of passion. Her body was moist all over. She felt a… and then she woke up.

Archie was giving Chloe last minutes instructions on how Camille likes to work. He was the numbers guy, and Camille was the front man. He had worked with Camille for years but was nervous about Chloe becoming a part of the team.

Up unto now Chloe's involvement in the company consisted of accompanying her father as an arm piece, attending social functions to represent the company, or just dropping in on her way to be pampered.

"*Today, your role will be to put out and pick up materials, I will be handling technology; Camille is the spoke person. She likes for handouts to be available for the attendee when they arrive. Did you get the refreshments packed?*" Asked Archie.

"*Yes, I can't believe how nervous I am. I brought fresh flowers for the refreshment table, and I thought a white tablecloth would look nice. Archie, could you get that folding table? I wasn't sure what space they would have for the refreshments.*" Said Chloe.

"*Man, you really are bringing class to the situation.*" Archie smiled.

"*Thanks.*" Before she knew it, her arms were around his neck. She quickly jumped away.

"I guess we better be going." Said Archie softly.

"Well, Ms. Ray how do you feel about your progress? Asked Sly.
"Good, I can see the different in some of my "Keep Hope Alive Clothes."
"Keep Hope Alive?"
"Yeah, those clothes you keep saying one day I am going to get back in to." Camille laughed.
"Good for you. So, how's your diet?" Asked Sly?
"Okay, I guess. Why do you ask?"
"Well because at some point I like to go grocery shopping with my clients to help them understand labels, and what to avoid, and help them stay on track." Is this something you think you would like?"
"Yeah, that would be nice. I must admit it can be like going through a mine field in the grocery store. I saw you and your wife in Safeway the other night, you and she seemed to be very intense. Do you always read the cans with such intensity?" asked Camille.
", I do read labels with intensity, but that was not my wife, it was a client that was having trouble with the diet end of her health journey...I didn't see you? Said Sly.
"Well, I was on my way out." Said Camille.
"Do you think you would like to have a shopping field trip? But you probably eat out a lot." So maybe we should go out for dinner to see how you are ordering." Sly suggested.
"Do all the trainers do this service, is it part of company policy? Or are you acting independently?" Camille Asked.
"Boy, you get right to the point. I'm acting independently, but if you are uncomfortable. I apologize to you. I never meant to make you feel uncomfortable."
"Oh, no! I must apologize to you! I don't have a filter sometimes. If the invitation is still open... I would love to be taught how to resist the garlic bread at Red Lobster." Camille said with a flirtatious smile.
"So, it's a date. I will meet you at Louise Restaurant on Griffin on tomorrow night around 7:30."

Chloe was taking her apprenticeship serious. She was reading and completing reports and going out to the businesses with Archie.
Camille had spoken with Archie about her progress, and he was extremely proud of her. She had noticed that the two of them

had been spending a lot of time together at work and outside of work. They were attending Wednesday Night Bible study, and church service on Sunday. She knew her father would be proud of his girls.

But her thought quickly turned to the concern of tonight. Camille had butterflies in her stomach. What would she be like by 7:30? She didn't know what she was going to wear.? Maybe she should go shopping for something causal, yet flirty. But Sly had not given any indication that he was interested in her that way. He was always professional during her sessions and personal conversation had been very limited. But she had to admit it… she was *"so hot"* for him! And that dream…What was that about?

She was unsure as to what tonight is about. Was this a date? Or Date?. If it was a DATE… she didn't want to blow it. She hated to admit it, but she needed the assistance of an expert.

Chloe tapped lightly on Camille's door; *"You wanted to see me?"*

"Yes, have a seat. I wanted to tell you. I think you have added to the presentations. I don't know how I ever made it without you." Camille said nicely.

"Well, I have to give credit to Archie, he's a great teacher."

"Archie? What's going on with you two these days?"

"Nothing, he's just so nice and patient with me. He listens to my thoughts and ideas. I really love working with him… and thank you for the chance to try to be better, than an old pageant queen." Chloe gave a modest smile.

They laughed and thought it had been a long time since they had laughed like sisters.

"Chloe, I called you in because I need your help. I think, I am going on a date tonight."

"A DATE? Who? What? Tell me! **Wait, what do you mean you think you are going on a date?**

"Well, I'm not sure, it's with my trainer, he said he is going to teach me how to order at a restaurant. So, I'm not sure is this is part of his training, or his way of asking me out. What do you think?"

"I think it is better to be safe than sorry. It is 10:15, we've got 7 hours cancel all your appointments. We've got work to do."

After hair and nails the sisters rushed Camille's closet to see if she had somethings fabulous because there was no time to go shopping.

"Don't worry the key to a great outfit is accessories." Said Chloe. This was her world. *"I'm sure you have something in your **"keep hope alive"** closet stash for a business/date date. I'm looking for something hot, where's that hot pink dress you wore two years ago for Daddy's birthday party? Asked Chloe.*

"It's probably in the back on the left. Both ladies were in the closet pulling and pushing their way through the massive mounds of clothing dating back like a history book of Camille's life.

Suddenly, there it was... the box. It was hidden in the back... push down like the memories and the emotion of that day that never was. The sisters carefully removed the box and laid it on the bed. They looked at it and without saying a word Camille slowly, picked it up and placed it back into the closet, into the abyss of the closet behind the mounds and mounds of useless clothing that cluttered Camille's closet and her life.

By 6:15 Camille looked like she was going to the prom. Every hair was in place every nail polished, makeup perfectly pretty, eyebrow plucked and arched; she was ready for her close- up. "Thanks sis, I would've looked like a hot mess." Said Camille.

"Well, it was fun. It has been a long time since we played dress up. Besides, I owe you one for giving me a chance to start my life over, and I am happier than I've ever been. So, get that man. If it is a date or not…. He will be the most envied man in that whole place tonight. BECAUSES SIS…YOU LOOK GOOD!

Camille had planned to be at the restaurant before Sly; but Chloe, **The Mistress of Seduction** corrected her ill-thought-out plan. Chloe suggested; he should wait a minimum of 15 minutes. Approach the restaurant as if Sly could see her arrival. Let her dress and hair flutter in the wind, while she tries to hold them in place. This gives off a look of helplessness, needing to be saved by a big strong man. She should make direct eye contact, then shyly look away, make him think his presence is too overpowering. Make him call your name when you do, acknowledge him, offer both your hands as a greeting, this is an act of submission Then go in for the kill; with the undereye look.

Camille's heart was beating a mile a minute as she tried to park the car. For some reason she could not get that darn car into that space. If Sly is watching, he probably thinks she's an idiot. Finally, the car was parked. It was time for her grand entrance. It worked! Just like Chloe said. Sly walked like he was ten feet tall, as he rescued his lady from the elements and delivered her safely to her seat.

"This is a very nice restaurant. I've heard of it; but this is my first time eating here." Said Camille.

"Really? I would have thought a business lady like you would know all the best places." Asked Sly.

"Well, to be honest I have not been that sociable for quite some time."

"Why is that?
"**Wow**! Are you trying to get into my head?" Camille was guarded.

"No… Do you ever get off defense? The one thing that I already know about you is that you are strong. But what I want you to know is that all of us, at some time are vulnerable, and it is not a sign of weakness, but a sign of just being human. We are here to help each other through tough times."

And with that Camille took a deep breath. After five long years she could finally let it go, and a single teardrop was proof that she had.

After that the conversation was effortless. Sly did do some teaching about ordering, but Camille heard very little of his instructions. She was still trying to figure out if this was a date or a business meeting, and how did he see her unhappiness, has everyone been able to read her emotions?

"Tell me Sly, has the company said anything about addressing childhood obesity? You know that the big buzz word these days." Said Camille.

Sly sat back. "I Can't believe this. I have been thinking on this very thing." I was thinking on a concept of a gym strictly for children. It would have the right size machines, classes that are age appropriated, I was thinking of calling it "New Tricks"

"New Tricks?"

"Yes, You can't teach an old dog new tricks, but you can teach a young pup, you get it.

Camille smiled, I get it, and I love it. Sounds like you want to be the Tyler Perry of fitness. I might be able to help you with it. Is this a dream Give me 2 weeks?

OKAY! You've got it! Sly smiled.

Sly walked her to her car and commented on her lousy parking. Camille had not laughed so much in one night in a very long time.

"Sly, how can I ever thank you for tonight. You will never know how much I have enjoyed myself. I really appreciate you."

She offered him both of her hands, just as Chloe had instructed. He took her hands, held them …and placed them around his neck… and wrapped his arms around her shrinking waist…pulled her close… and kissed her softly on the lips…slowly… than hard. It was a DATE!

How was Camille supposed to get her head down from the clouds? All she could think of was this was the night she fell in love. But she was scared. She didn't want to lose focus and miss signs like she had with Jonathan. Did Sly do this with all his female clients?

Why me? She asked herself."

"Knock, Knock. "So how was the date? I waited for you to call me."
"Oh, it was fine."
"Well?"
"Well, What?"
I can tell when someone is telling me to butt out…Anyway, Archie will be here with mom in a minute. We've got something to tell both of you.

Archie and Esther came in and everyone took a seat. Archie took Chloe's hand, Camille and Esther looked puzzled.

"Mrs. Mac, Camille I have been with this family for a long time. Mr. Mac was very good to me. He treated me like a son. If he were here, I would ask his permission to marry his daughter, but he is not …Mrs. Mac, Camille I would like your approval to make Chloe my wife."

The room erupted in Mayhem. Tears and hugs were everywhere. *"I must admit that this got pass me."* Said Esther. *"Mac would be so proud to call you, his son."*

Camille was happy for her baby sister, and Archie. Actually, she was not that surprised. Archie had always been fascinated with Chloe. He seemed to see her as fragile, and delicate. Chloe had always shown her vulnerability through her femininity.

"Okay, you two, try to be down from cloud nine by two this afternoon. I have a couple of things I would like to share with you." Said Camille.

The happy couple left the office hand and hand.

Esther stayed. *"I couldn't be happier for those two. Well, how is the undercover exercising going?"* Camille held up her arms. *"You tell me!"*

I like what I see. Anything developing on your undercover work?"
"I'm working on something. Said Camille.

Esther took a seat across from her daughter.

"Camille, I want to talk to you. I recently realized something that I must share with you. That day Jonathan came to us about the situation with the girl being pregnant. **I went crazy!** *I was so out of control that day. You had to be the voice of reason. You calmed the room down. You comforted Jonathan and his mother, and you calmed me down.*

After that you notified and cancelled everything. You shouldn't have had to do that. I know now that I took that very emotional moment from you and made it all about me. I was angry about something that happened way before you were even born. I didn't allow you to grieve your loss. I did not comfort you the way a mother should have…On that day I saw life go out of your eyes. So, I am asking for your forgiveness… and I hope you can finally be angry, upset, vindictive, whatever it takes to make you feel whole, so that you can move on with your life. You deserve to be happy."

Camille came from her desk and into her mother's arms and softly wept.

Archie and Chloe were back in Camille's office around two that afternoon.
"Well, are you two back down to earth?" They smiled.
"The reason I wanted to see you both is I want to make a proposal for a business, and I need your help. **Maximum Impact** as you know is the gym where I've been working out. Overall, it is set up fairly well. I need for you two to go over and get a feel of the place. Also, I would like for you to do some research on children's gyms. See if there are any out there, and if so, what are they like? "Let's plan to sit down by Friday for preliminary discussion and planning."
"Well, it looks like we are getting in shape for the wedding. Should we ask for your trainer?"
"No, just go in and get an honest feel of the place, don't mention your association with me or the firm. "I want you to see the gym as it is." "Before you go, I guess you two will be planning a wedding. You know this town is growing in the entertainment field. I think this would be a great time to kick off our new **Event Planning Division**. Keep in mind everyone will be watching If the **Head of the Division** makes a mess of their own wedding. I don't think that would be good for business." The couple smiled.
"Alright, we will get right on it. "Archie left the room, but Chloe stayed behind. "Sis, you look different. You look happy. The sisters embraced "I am," said Camille.

Chloe and Archie wasted no time. The plan was to mingle with the clients to see how they viewed the gym. Chloe was dressed very cute and got male attention right away. She was helped on every machine she worked out on. This certainly was a meat market she thought as she watched the ladies checking out Archie. Dino approached her as she tried to figure out how to operate one of the machines.
"Well, you must be new, My name is Dino, I am one of the trainers here. Can I help you?"
"Yes, that would be very nice of you. Thanks," said Chloe.
"I can see that you know how to take care of your body...You look really familiar. Have you been here before?" He asked.
Just then Camille came through the door.
"Excuse me. **HEY Thomas!** He motioned his head to the door of which Camille was coming through. "Look like Sly was right. It is March 1." Chloe looked confused, "What are you talking about?"

Oh, nothing, just a little bet we made on January 2nd that before March 1 some of our newly signed up clients would have marched right back to their comfy couch. You see I have a theory. Some people worship their bodies and some…well just wear their bodies out." He chuckled.

Chloe jumped off the machine and stomped off to the locker room to retrieve Camille. "Camille, Camille, let's get out of this dump!

As Camille stared out at the city from her condo's windows, Chloe sat on the sofa, not knowing what to say. She had just done the most painful thing she had ever had to do. She had to watch her sister's heart be broken once again.

Thoughts were running through Camille's mind. *So, that was why he was so attentive about her workouts. It was all so he could win some stupid bet. How could she have been so wrong about him?* She thought he was a man of substance. But he was quite a chameleon. What would her next move be? Could she show her face at that gym again? Maybe happiness wasn't meant for her. What was that dinner about?

The doorbell rang. It was Archie. Hey, I got your text. Chloe was upset and started to cry. Archie was comforting her.

Camille slowly turned from the window; *"What the hell are you two doing? This is not about you! This is about me. If anyone should be upset or comforted* **"IT'S ME!"** **No one betted against you! Or called you a loser. Go Home…I am going to be just fine. I'm always Just fine!**

Archie collected Chloe, and gently touched Camille on the shoulder and whispered, *"I am just a phone call away."*

Just then her phone rang. It was Sly, she did not answer. She was still figuring things out.

The next morning Camille got ready for work. She took her black suit from the cleaner bag and slipped on the skirt, and it nearly fell to the floor. She was in shock. She was not the same girl she was two months ago physically or emotionally. She had changed and she was not going back!

She searched in the closet through that mountain of clothes, some of which she had not worn in years. A red mini she had worn only once was calling her name. It was a little much for the office; but she didn't care. She needed this…It was the first day of the new Camille's life. She felt rejuvenated and empowered.

Her assistance face said it all without saying a word.

"Good morning, Ms. MacMillan.

Camille was in full makeup, and every hair was in place. She was wearing stilettos and carrying a smoothie in her Nutri-Bullet cup. Good morning, Her phone was ringing as she walked through her office door. "Hello,"

"Well, hello Ms. Mac. This is Elon Steele; I hope you haven't forgotten me."
"No, I haven't. Said Camille.
"You did receive your letter with the details?"
"Yes, I did." Said Camille.
"I'm calling to confirm the cover shoot for the June issue of WBL.
Do you have your own people, or do we need to set up a glam team for you?"
"I'll use your people."
"Good, then we will see you 10:30 Thursday morning The address is on the letter."
"That sounds fine, I'll see you then.
Esther stepped inside the door of Camille's office. May I come in?
"Of Course!"
"How are you today?"
"I'm fine."
"Well, I must say you look fine too…a red mini skirt for the office. I like it."
"Your sister told me about what happen at the gym… I wish I had never given you that certificate, baby I'm sorry."
"Sorry for what? Mom look at me. Life has it rough, and stumble, I'm fine." "Look at me, don't look fine… "Did Chloe and Archie tell you tell you that they are getting married the last Saturday in June? And the Women In Business Banquet is the 3rd Friday of June. June is going to be a busy month."
"OH, I am working on a presentation for **MI** gym."
"Well, your plate is full."
"Camille, before I let you get back to work. I'm thinking about moving to Savannah. I feel like I need to start over. The house has too many memories and feel that is my old life. I need to understand my new life as Esther MacMillan…widow. Your auntie and I can watch after one another. Just like I want you and Chloe to do when you are our age."
"You don't need me to run this house."
"Mom. What are we going to do without you?"
"You are going to be just fine! I'm just a phone call away."

Camille checked her calendar. Sure, enough she had a session with Sly, and she was going. But she had a stop she needed to make on her way.
"Good afternoon, Welcome to **Work It Out Fitness**, how can I help you?"
"I am interested in active wear for children. But first I am looking for some new workout gear for myself…Oh and do you monogram?"
Camille traded in her big tee and baggy sweatpants for a pair of black leggings with a hot stripe on the side, and a sleeveless pink and black tee that said what else…"Just Do It" with the New **MI** LOGO.

Camille took a deep breath and pushed open the gym door. She knew that Sly probably knew nothing about the incident, and she had decided not to confront him for now. In a way she may have the upper hand. She was going to show him what he was never going to get. Besides, this was business, she wasn't going to lose a potential client for some low-level trainer. But she would use him to get to that "Monday" meeting. Who know, if she can help this business franchise, it could be very profitable for Perfect Image.

"Well, Who do we have here?"

"What?" Camille asked.

"You look different today?" Sly smiled.

"Really, Let's get pumped. I've got a lot of energy today. So, make me sweat." Camille pulled out her limited seductive arsenal. She intentionally rubbed up against him, every chance she got. She tossed her hair, wiped her chest, and expressed how hot she was. When they were finished, she had released a lot of toxins both physical and emotional. After thinking about what Chloe had said. Sly had betted on her, not against her… and for now she was going to stand on the relationship for what it had been.

"*Sly, do you think you could get me inside that* **Monday morning** *meeting with the gym owner. I have some things I would like to share with the company about franchising… and I could introduce your idea of the children gym, and of course I will give you credit for your idea.*"

Sly raised one eyebrow, and said, "*I think I can make that happen. I'll will call you with the details. Good workout. Well, there is my next client.*"

"And to think, it is March 3," Camille Smiled.

"Excuse Me?"

"Take care, call me."

"We need to talk."

Later that evening Camille got a text: **Monday 10:00am, Sleep Sweet!**

Chloe and Archie were fabulous; graphics, background, projections visual, everything she needed for this presentation to be the best one she had ever done. The three of them worked like ants all week. She could not wait to see Sly's face when he sees the other side of her.

"Camille, can you go dress shopping with me this Saturday?"

"Of course, I wouldn't miss it for the world. You are going to make a beautiful bride." Is Archie coming too?"

"Nooo it's bad luck for the groom to see the dress." Snarled Chloe.

"Didn't help very much in my case." Camille chuckled.

"But he didn't ever see the dress." Chuckled Chloe.

"Nor did anyone else." They both laughed.

This was the first time they had ever shown any emotion about that situation."

"You know I think Archie should come; he is your best friend. He's like a brother to me and you value his opinion."

"As long as he doesn't go all DIVA on us.....Why not."

"Well Archie, you in? Asked Chloe.

"I was hoping you would ask." He responded in his best DIVA voice.

"Let's meet for breakfast at Marietta Diner before the appointment." Said Archie.

"If you're paying, I'm in. said Camille.

"You're not going to fit in any dress after the big ass omelet that you just ate."

"You're one to talk, you ate three pancakes the size of frisbee, with sausage."

They were all laughing and teasing Chloe as the fumbled through the doors of **Vows and Veils Bridal Boutique.**

"Welcome to V&V, the hostess seated them on a Tiffany Blue Chippendale sofa and gave them champagne.

"I'm Laura and I will be your personal stylist. Tell me what you are looking for today?"

Chloe described to Lauren what she was looking for in a wedding dress.

Camille was thinking...*what a cheesy introduction...champagne, how clique.*

Chloe was taken away by Lauren to a dressing room.

"Why did Chloe come back to this shop? There are other Bridal shops in this town." Whispered Esther.

"Because they're cheap. Archie and Camille said together. They snickered like two mischievous fifth graders.

"You two stop it...I'm just saying." Said Esther.

"Mom stop it!... Let it go. I'M fine. Beside that you're paying for her dress, so you should be happy she came here." Smiled Camille.

Finally, Chloe came out in a dress. Too much at the bottom... the next dress, didn't have enough on top, the third dress... too slutty for a church service, fourth dress... just too too... nothing seemed to work.

Cho, I'm tired, I need a nap, and this champagne isn't helping any, said Esther.

"Me too, whined Camille, Let's come back."

"Yeah, I don't think we should have gone to Breakfast." Said Archie. "Next time let's not do breakfast."

"We have to find a dress today guys, stop messing around. Eight weeks is not a long time."

"Chloe we've got time. I promise I will come back, and I will stay focused. Said Camille.

"You know my eye lids are attached to my belly." Said Esther.

"I feel like a big old tick that's about to pop. Said Archie.

"You three are worthless. Lauren, I'm sorry. But I will be back, and I am leaving this mutinous crew at home. Thank you for your patience and hospitality." Said Chloe.

"No problem, I get sleepy when I eat too. Take Care and come back we will be here."

"Why did I Bring Larry, Curly, and Moe to help me look for a gown. Let's go. I can show you the things I pulled for your cover shoot. At least the day won't be a total waste."

"Drop me off at home. I'm sleepy." Esther yawned.

Monday was finally here, and Camille was in her office praying, really praying, not those quick repetitive prays that she said every night before bed; but a pray of connection to God; asking for his guidance and clarity. She had done presentations that were worth thousands of dollars; but this felt like the most important presentation she had ever made. Chloe and Archie came into her office.

"We're packed and ready to go."

"Come in, have a seat. Today I will do the introduction to the presentation, and you two will bring it home. Archie of course you will handle the numbers, and Chloe you will explain the visual and design.

I will be there to quarter back when needed. Chloe, stop looking scare. You are the smartest Christmas ornament I know. And Archie is the wind beneath your wings. It's time for you to FLY!"

By 9:45 everything was set up, projection reports, cost analysis, visuals. Refreshment table.

Sly walked in, followed by Dino, Thomas, and James. Sly took the chair at the head of the table. Camille looked at the door, then she looked at Sly sitting in the head chair and fingers interlocked, waiting to be impressed. Had she missed something?

Well, at this point she had to play the hand she was dealt and do what she does best, tell a story. Chloe had the team dressed in workout gear with the

New Logo for **MI**. *She introduced the slogan;* **No Mission is Impossible at Maximum Impact.**

Chloe presented the importance of merchandising; things like keychains, water bottles, clothing and a host of items would make clients feel like they are part of an exclusive club. Camille planted the seed; as distasteful as it sounds; *Human like to have someone to look down on.* And being a part of **MI Fitness Center would be the envy of every gym rat in the nation.**

Archie followed with impressive visuals and number crunching. Chloe addressed design and flow of facility. She suggested a juice bar café. Of course, Chloe was the face for the ads Tee shirt, posters, for the company store. A portfolio was presented for **New Tricks Children Fitness Center** for Sly to review. Sly sat stone face throughout the presentation.

When everything was finished, Sly and the others had questions. Overall, they were impressed with **Perfect Image Consultant Agency** and said they would review the information and get back to them.

"But before we leave the table there are a few personal matters that we need to clear up." Said Sly.

"Dino, I think you have something you need to say." Sly said sternly.

"Chloe, I was stupid and unprofessional. I will never talk about a client like that again. I regret that you heard that about your sister.

"Camille, I don't know of anything I could say to take away the vulgarity of us betting on your failure. Let me make myself clear, Sly chastised us, and left the room before any of that childish behavior took place. All I can do is ask for your forgiveness. I want you to know that Sly is one of a kind.

When he had the opportunity for this place, he brought us in as partners, he took three lowly trainers and made businessmen out of us. I will be forever grateful to him." Dino's apology seemed sincere. He is a good man.

Chloe and Archie packed up for their departure. Camille was at one end of the conference table and Sly was at the other end. Did Camille need Chloe to tell her what to say to do? Should she jump on top of the table and run and leap into his arms or should she stay put and let him come to her. This was still a business meeting and maybe she should finish it as one. Chloe and Archie shook Sly's hand and left the conference room.

Now they were alone in the room. They began to move slowly to the center.

"Well, why didn't you tell me you were the CEO of Maximum Impact, and who is Lee Sanford?" Asked Camille.

"You never asked; and I am Lee Sanford. I dropped my first name and used my middle name."

"**Smart Move**" Sylvester Lee would not play well in the business world. Camille Laughed. "I am sorry that I doubted your character…I should have had more faith in you, or at least had the guts to give you a chance to explain.

"Well, that should have never happened, but I think it made them grow up. So, something good did come out of it. Besides, I liked the way you worked out your frustration at our last workout."

"So are we still strictly business. Asked Camille. "I mean you must meet so many beautiful women. Why me?"

"It was your mother."

"My mother?"

"Yes, when she came in to buy the certificate. She spoke about her daughter; how beautiful she was inside and out; but that you were going through a hard time and that you need a chance to start again. So, I marked your certificate so that I would give you special attention when and if you came in. But when you walked through the door that day you stole my heart just as you were. I could see you were a woman of substance…. And then I saw the certificate I knew that you were meant to be in my life." Sly took her into his arms and held her close.

Camille called Chloe over to her apartment. "Chloe, I was thinking back to when you were describing to the clerk what you were looking for in a dress. She took her little sister by the hand and led her to the bedroom door., and there in the middle of the floor was the dress that she had described to Lauren just days ago in the bridal shop.

"I got your model stand from mom. I only got it because you said it was the one. This is the way you want to look on your wedding day."

"Oh Camille, I always thought it was such a beautiful dress to never to be seen. You're willing to give me your dress?" It was never my dress. **SO**, are you saying yes to the dress?"

"**YES, YES, YES,**"!

Camille was exhausted between work, Chloe's wedding, her mother relocating and a new relationship, everything was upside down. But there was one more event that need her attention.

The June Edition of WBL magazine was finally out; and she must admit. SHE LOOKED GOOD! Camille McMillian a cover model, her father would have never believed it. The banquet was in a few days, and she was expected to give a speech. She was a little nervous because her audience had always been small. But It felt good to know that she would have the support of her family and of Sly. She never thought that happiness would find its way back into her life.

The night of the banquet Camille looked gorgeous. Chloe had found the perfect outfit for her. It had been a long time since she had a night like this. Her doorbell rang and when she answered there was Chloe, Archie, Esther, and Sly with champagne and glasses.
"Cinderella, your chariot has arrived." Said Archie.
"Well, it should be a carriage not a chariot; but as long as my Prince Charming is here... I will ride on the back of a milk truck."
"Everyone come in I'm ready. I just need to get my purse and speech."
"No, we each should make a toast to this occasion first." Said Esther.
They held up their glasses.
"To Big Mac, he would be proud of both his daughters tonight, and his soon to be sons in law."
"Mom!" Camille shrieked.
"Well, I want to be a grandmother!"
Archie lifted his glass.
"To my beautiful bride to be, I love you more and more each day, and to my new mom and sister, thank you for your respect and always treating me like family. I love all of you, and Sly welcome to the family."
"Wow, Big Sis, I have always looked up to you, you have the biggest heart of anyone I know. You always put everyone else before yourself.
You are my woman of the year every day. Thank you for giving me a chance to begin again, and Archie. I have always loved you. But I thought you could never be interested in a girl like me. But you saw something in me that I didn't see in myself. Thank you for loving me."
"I'm proud to be part of this wonderful family, Camille I can't think of a better time than this. He reached into his pocket and whipped out a contract. *"Will you franchise with me in New Trick Fitness Center for Children?"*
Everyone laughed.
"The next time it better be a ring." Esther said in a mother's voice.
Camille raised her glass.
"My head is spinning and it's not from the champagne... I am happy. I am happy with my family, my new brother-in-law, my sister and my mom and my new boyfriend. If anyone would have told me just six months ago that I would have a second chance for happiness I would have never believed them. Here's to Love, Peace, Happiness, and SECOND CHANCE!"

Illusions

Camille awoke in her childhood bedroom. It had been a long time since she had slept there in this safe place. She reflected on the blessing and the curse of being the daughters of Mac and Esther's McMillian.

They had been raised in somewhat of a cocoon. They rarely attended birthday parties or sleepovers, unless they were daughters of some prominent member of the community. They attended such functions as *Jack and Jill Ball*. *The Mayor's Ball*, or some political functions. They attended private school so as to nurture their perspective futures, engineered by their father.

Chloe came in and jumped in her bed. "I'm getting married today!" Camille GET UP!

"Girl you better get out of here." She looked at her little sister, she looked so happy. It must be wonderful to find your one true love. She hoped that she would too. But her relationship with Sly was a new and at times awkward. Chloe and Archie had decided to wait until they were married to have sex, but Sly and she were like rabbits. The sex was GOOD... but **their intimacy needed work.**

"Okay, I'm up!"

"Hurry up Mom is cooking breakfast for us. She and Aunt Ruth are waiting for you."

Camille came down in her robe and took her seat at the table. Aunt Ruth was mom's sister. She lived in Savannah. Like Esther, she had lost her life partner about four years ago. She rarely came to Atlanta anymore; but she was here for Chloe's wedding.

Camille kissed her mother and auntie on the cheek, "Good morning."

"Good morning to you did you sleep okay?"

"Yes, I had forgotten how good that bed feels."

"Well, if you like, you can take it with you, or I can put it in storage for you."

Chloe and Camille looked puzzled.

"WHAT?" I told both of you I was thinking of moving to Savannah. I don't need this big house. I never did, this is your daddy's idea. I just moved in."

"Okay, enough about that. Let's just talk about happy stuff. Let's talk about me. I'm so glad I decided to do a small ceremony. The bottom line is I only want those closest to us to be there. The glam team will be here soon to make all of us more beautiful."

New Jerusalem Baptist Church was respected in the city. Its membership was made up of middle-class families, mostly African American. In the past the Mac Millian family showed up every Sunday because it was the thing that successful families did. But to tell the truth Camille could not remember ever seeing her father or mother reading the Bible, and after the embarrassment of the wedding her father no longer felt comfortable showing his face.

Once again, the doors of New Jerusalem Baptist Church had opened for a Mac Millian union. Five years ago, it didn't happen, but today it is decorated beautifully; it was a place of redemption for this family.

Pastor Bryant Jackson was the son of the previous pastor. Camille really didn't know him that well. Archie and Chloe were quite taken with him. She knew that there had been some controversy because his wife was the first winner in a new lottery game that he had so vigorously protested.

Chloe looked beautiful in her gown. She walked down the aisle with her mother by her side. Camille had preceded them as her one and only bridesmaid. Events like this reminded Camille of the sheltered life that she and Chloe had lived. They had no real friends. But Chloe through Archie seem to be expanding his relationships with the good church people.

Camille had hoped that they would have thrown a more eloquent event, it would have been great for the new event planning division.

But this quaint get together would generate little or no business buzz. Sly had agreed to be her date for the reception, although it would not be much of a celebration. They had elected to use the church's fellowship hall, which meant a tamed party. Still, it was good to know she would have someone to hold on to.

Camille, Camille, Mac Millian? I know you probably do not remember me; I am Cynthia Peterson Jackson now.

"Yes." *The two ladies embraced.*

"It's been years, you look beautiful. You really have maintained your figure. You look good."

"I have to thank my trainer, Sly, this is Cynthia Jackson. Her husband is the Pastor"

I need to get busy getting in shape, those desk jobs will ruin your figure." Said Cynthia.

"Well, I highly recommend him. He is the owner and CEO of Maximum Impact Gym/Spa.

"Nice to meet you. Did she say spa, boy that sounds great?"

Cynthia? You work with the school system? Asked Camille.

"Yes, I'm a counselor"

"Sly, she may be able to help us. Cynthia, what are your thoughts on Childhood Obesity?

"Well, it is a big problem."

"The reason I asked is that Sly is working on a new gym concept geared to children 7 to 17. It is in the planning stages, and we could use your insight. What are you doing Monday around 4:00pm? We can make it a spa day. Said Camille.

"And well deserved after this school year. "Said Cynthia.

"Great, do you know where Maximum Impact is located?"

"I'll find it. It was good seeing you again. Nice meeting you Sly." Cynthia left the table.

Sly turned to Camille, *"What are you doing? I would appreciate it if you would consult with me before you do something like that...I don't know that a woman and I don't trust preachers."*

"Oh, they are good people. Her mother and my mother use to work together."

"Good people, so you say, don't do that again. I'm very careful with who I let into my business."

He gave Camille the silent treatment for the remainder of the reception. The potato salad wasn't the only thing that was cold.

Chloe and Archie had decided to postpone their honeymoon because they wanted to be present for the next Quarterly Financial Report Meeting.

This would be the Event Planning Division first report. Esther was in from Savannah to attend the meeting. She sat at one end of the conference table, and Camille at the other. Archie sat on Esther's right side for the meeting and placed Chloe to Esther's left. This did not go unnoticed by Camille. Archie sat by her at the last meeting. Is this the beginning of a new alliance?

The meeting opened and flowed easily as each company reported their expenditure, intake, profit margins and projections for the next quarter. Finally, it was Archie's time to shine. His report was precise and presented well. It was made clear that the Events Planning Division was in its planning stage.

"Well, I understand that Events is new, basically... I only heard about the expense of your new office. Can you tell me when this division will show a profit, and share with us how you intend to make this happen?" Asked Camille.

Archie fumbled. *"You, you, are right. We felt we must have an attractive place to bring in clients to reassure them that we have high standards. Also, it takes time to assemble vendors and clear them as businesses we want to be associated with... It also takes time to build a directory of venues.*

"We don't expect to be doing parties at Chuckie Cheese Camille. This division will not be a mickey mouse operation." He sat down abruptly.

Esther stood and said, *"Well I think this concludes this quarter's report. Thank all of you for the hard work you do. Remember this is A family business...and* **WE ARE FAMILY.**

After everyone had left Esther asked Camille to come to her end of the table.
"Well girls the house sold."
"Already?"
"Yes, I told you if you wanted anything from there you better come and get it. I'm going to give most of it to charity." *She gave both girls a key.* "You have about thirty days before closing. *Archie hugged Esther and left the room without saying a word to Camille, Chloe followed with the same.*

Camille stood to leave also. Esther gave Camille a stern motherly eye.
"What?"
"Sometimes you can be so much like your father. His sign was Leo, and so is yours. "Put your claws back in kitty cat."
"What are you talking about Mom?" *Camille said as if she was innocent.*
"You are a lot of things little girl, but stupid isn't one of them. If you are going to be the leader, then lead. A leader does not play childish games at Quarterly meetings. Like it or not Archie is family now and you may need him sooner than later. And that is all I have to say on that matter. What is going on with you and Sly?"
"He's my trainer and he's a friend."

Esther sat back in her chair. "A word of advice...35-year-old women, don't need 35-year-old male friends. If he is not going to sh—. Then he should get off the pot. Take it from me, if a man hangs around in your life with worthless intensions, he will bring you nothing but heartache... and frankly, you have had enough of that. "Now give your mother a hug." She popped Camille's bottom.

"Ouch, that hurt!"

"I meant for it too! Said Esther.

Camille went to the gym for her training with Sly. The workout had gone okay, but she was not feeling so well.

Lately, her period had become more painful, and lasting longer with a heavier flow.

"Camille, Let's get numbers." She stepped on the scale, "Camille, you've gained 4lbs."

"What, well, it's my cycle." Camille pouted.

"Okay, but you are up 7lbs. overall. Are you eating on plan?" He asked.

"I am not a child. I know what I'm suppose to do. Snapped Camille.

"When is your next doctor's appointment? If you don't have one makes one soon. If you are eating on plan, then something is going on. Have bloodwork done and get back to me. My client is here. Oh, I need for you to go with me on Wednesday to see this building I think you'll like."

As Sly walked away Camille was furious; she thought to herself, *no Good job! Good workout, Nothing*! She went out front and found that Cynthia had arrived early.

"I'm so glad you were able to make it. I have massages set up for us, let's go."

"Girl, I have been looking forward to this since you mention it. The truth is I needed a mini getaway, after the week I've had." Cynthia said.

Archie was seeing red. He walked into his newly decorated, newly designed office. He was due for an upgrade. He had been in the same cubby hole for 10 years. He needed his surrounding to correlate with his new position and new standing in the company.

Besides, he and Chloe were sharing the space, and that was good for now. Because he needed to mold her to take **their** proper place in the business and stop gazing upon Camille as if she was this *Great Wizard of Business*. That magazine cover had gone to her head.

He could not deny his recent resentment toward Camille. Lately, he seemed to have an urgency to take control from her. He didn't like these feelings, but they were there.

Archie had studied at Emory's MBA program just like Camille and Jonathan. They were all interns at the Mac Millian Corporate while in program. All three were offered positions after graduation. Now here he was 14 years later playing second fiddle to Camille.

He had hoped to be CEO of a fortune five hundred company by now. Some of his friends and family warned him not to get caught up with this small potato operation. But at the time opportunities for young black males were limited. Plus, he had interned with Mr. Mac throughout his program, and he respected him. His hands-on approach to growing a business was like food for the belly. He often said, "*take care of your people, and they will take care of your business.*"

Plus, Chloe was a joy to be around, even though she didn't know he was alive back then.

He had been a part of the rise of this empire, and he was not about to walk away empty handed. Camille may have birthright, but he was now a watchman for Chloe's rights to her seat on throne alongside of Camille.

Besides, Mr. Mac made it clear that he wanted him to run this business. The only drawback was it was a package deal. Camille would have to be at his right side as his wife. Thank God that she and Jonathan were like two peas in a pod, while he gazed upon the lovely Chloe from afar.

Mr. Mac, the masterful puppeteer was unable to make any of his puppets to come under his demands. Now his early demise had complicated things. When Jonathan and Camille didn't make it down the aisle he had to regroup. Mr. Mac often exposed his masterful plan, and it had remained on the table up until his death.

His plan for Chloe was a doctor or lawyer, but certainly not him. But his marriage to Chloe had upped his status and dream of running this company. He could finally make his move… Event Planning Division… No Thanks…It's all or nothing.

Camille and Cynthia are lying on the massage tables across from one another. "*So, Cynthia I was thinking you would be interested in a project from the ground up. This project certainly needs an educator, or someone with an understanding of children. Maybe you could serve on the Board Of Directors, as a consultant between the schools and the gym.*" Have you ever consider doing anything outside of the school setting?"

"You know Camille, I'm flattered that you would consider me. I must admit I have been wondering whether or not I want to spend 30 years in the public schools like our mothers. I wonder if this nicely packaged life as the preacher's wife and school counselor is enough. Plus, I want my daughter to dream bigger. *Board Of Directors*, it sounds so important."

"*You would probably use skills you don't even know you have. Take it from me, in life you need challenges, or you will stagnate; and one day you will look up and wonder where has all the time gone? Think about it, I know you have to run it by your husband. You've got time, we're just getting started.*"

"Girl, I can already tell you what Bryant is going to say. But I'm at a point that the obedient wife role is getting old. Hey, I know we are not girlfriends or anything. But what's the story with Sly, **that's one fine brother.**" "I don't know, we are friends, and he is my trainer. Now we are involved in this business venture, and I am not sure if you should mix the two. Dealing with men in the business world is rough. If a girl is to survive, she had better grow a set."

"A set?" asked Cynthia.

"You know…Balls" Camille smiled.

"That's not the first time I've been told that. Said Cynthia.

Chloe and Archie were finally on their honeymoon cruise. They were excited to have 7 days and nights of marriage delight.

"Honey, thank you for the way you had my back the other day at the Quarterly; I don't know what came over me. I hope I didn't disappoint you with my behavior." Said Archie.

"Camille started that, she's like that sometimes. She doesn't mean anything by it. She has always been focused like that. She strikes like a cobra, quick and swift. But she is a wonderful person."

"Chloe, sometimes you put Camille on a pedestal. But, you have just as much to offer. You know your daddy created **Perfect Image** for you. I wish he could have seen how impressed those guys were with your presentation for the gym, and with my help you are only going to get better; maybe even better than Camille."

He pulled her close into his arms as they watched the sun set across the water with the ocean winds blowing through their hair.

Camille hated it when Sly was right. She often felt that she was in competition with him. He thought he knew as much as she did about business. After all who was the one with a business degree. He had just got lucky with one business concept, and she was finding it difficult to advise him.

But this time he was right, she needed to see a doctor. Lately her cycle had been doing some funky things.

"Hi Doctor Brooks."

"Hi Camille, It has been a minute since I saw you, what brings you in today.""

"Well, I have been having severe pain with my cycle and a heavier than normal flow."

"Okay, before we do exam, let me just ask you a few questions Have you had your mammogram?"

"No, But I will schedule one as soon as I leave here today."

"Are, you sexually active?"

"Yes."

"Okay, what form of BC are you using?"

"BC? birth control, condoms and gels"

"Okay lay back, does it hurt here?" "After a few minutes, the doctor had Camille sit up.

"It is either one or two things and it can be both. But we won't know it until we do an ultrasound and a laparoscopy."

"Laparoscopy?"

"That's procedure where a small incision is made in the belly, and I can look around and if needed we can treat birth control pills.

"Birth control pills...Dr. Sandy, I don't think my sexual activity warrants me taking a pill every day. Until recently, I rarely have sex."

"The pill in this case would mainly be a treatment for the heavy bleeding and pain associated with fibroids, or endometriosis...it will balance out your hormones level.

"This brings me to another question. Are you planning to have children?"

"Yes, I would like to have at least one."

"Well make it a priority. Your clock is seriously ticking."

After leaving the doctor's office Camille was not really that shocked. She suspected she had fibroids. They are common among black females, but she was not familiar with endometriosis. Nor had she given much thought about motherhood. She assumed she was doomed to the life of an old maid. "OLD MAID? Where did that come from? But now Sly changed everything, motherhood could be back on the table.

Where is this darn place Sly wanted her to see? She thought.

Here, I guess this is it. In front of the building stood Sly and a tall guy, probably the real estate agent. The closer she got he looked more and more familiar. She stopped the car and shut the engine off. She could feel her body go limp, even though she was sitting. She knew she had to get out of the car.

"Oh Lord please let my legs hold me up, and please Lord help me not to pee on myself."

She slowly got out of the car and took a deep breath. Sly said, Camille, this is Jonathan Edward. He is going to show us this building, I think you will like it."

Camille extended her hand to Mr. Edwards His touch set her mind searching like high-speed internet.

The last time she saw him flash quickly through her mind.

Throughout the entire tour, she engaged in conversation about the vision of the kid's gym. But she really had no idea what she said. At one point Sly walked away from Camille and Jonathan; and Jonathan quickly handed Camille his card.

"Please call me we need to talk."

"We have nothing to talk about."

Just as Sly rejoined them Jonathan asked, "So what do you think?"

"I love it!" I think it is just what we had in mind."

Jonathan handed Sly and Camille a card. "Take some time, talk about it, and give me a call. But I will say this with the economy picking up, buildings like this, that match up to what you are looking for, will go fast." With that the meeting was over and Jonathan left.

Sly walked Camille to her car. "How did the doctor's visit go?"

"Okay, but there is a concern. I'm scheduled to have a procedure on Friday. It is an outpatient procedure. Do you think you could go with me?""

"Let me check my calendar, and I will get back to you. I've got to get back to the gym." Camille was sure what to think as she drove away from the two most frustrating men she had ever known.

Camille's Home

Camille's phone rang, it was Jonathan. How did he get her number? Should she answer it? Why open up old wounds? She did have some unanswered questions. The phone rang four times, five times, six times, finally she answered and said…nothing.

"Camille, I'm glad you picked up."

"What do you want?"

"Please meet me at the IHOP on 75 South. What I have to say to you has to be said in person." *Silence.*

"Afterward I promise I will never bother you again. 7:30
CLICK.

Camille had wondered, what had gone so horribly wrong? They had been so happy together. And then in one night it had all gone away.

She picked up the phone and pressed redial and said.

"I'll be there."

Camille came through the door of the IHOP. Jonathan stood to greet her. She had avoided looking at him earlier that day. She had forgotten how attractive he is. Tall slender with Nestle Chocolate brown smooth skin, and she did love chocolate. His close-cut hair complimented his manner of dress. Coordinated as if taken directly off a department store mannequin. That was his style.

"I can't tell you how many times I have lived this moment in my head. Thank you for coming. This conversation has been six years in the making."

"First, let me say you look wonderful, I saw the WIB cover, and I said why didn't I fight for this girl?"

Camille took a deep breath, and said, Did You love me?"

Jonathan leaned forward and took her hand, **"Yes, and I still do. After all this time no one has taken your place in my heart."**

Puzzled, Camille asked **"What went wrong?"** *I never suspected you were seeing someone else."*

"I was younger than, and maybe I didn't know how to let you know what I needed from you. Remember, one evening were working on a project for your father. As I recall it wasn't due the next day. But you wanted to finish it that evening to impress your father...I wanted to go to IHOP. I started kissing you on your neck, just messing around with you when **"YOU SNAPPED!"** *and said,* **"If you want to leave, then leave!"**

"I lost my temper and ended up at the Waffle House. There was this young woman sitting in the booth. She was wearing headphones enjoying her music and food. She reminded me of you and how carefree you can be at times, but at the same time you could have fangs, like a pitbull. This woman reminded me of the Camille that I loved carefree, happy. We made eye contact and struck up a conversation.

I'm not proud of it, but we hooked up that night, and two more times. I hated how I felt. I don't understand how people cheat. But I caught myself and came to my senses.

A few weeks later she called to say she was pregnant. She seemed like a nice lady from a nice family, I had no reason to doubt her. I knew we were only a few weeks away from our wedding. I talked to my mother, and she told me I had to confess my fall and ask for your forgiveness. She came with me as my support, but mostly to keep your father from choking life out of me." They both laughed. "But it wasn't your father…who knew that a dignified lady like your mother could show her hindy like she did. But it wasn't even her reaction that shock me...**It was yours.**"

Camille looked surprised.

"I wasn't sure if you were relieved or what? You were so calm and kind, gave me permission to do the right thing, and that you would handle calling off the wedding. You even assured me that everything was going to be alright. Basically, it was like you were relieved to have a way out. No one was happy in that room that evening except for your Dad. He never liked me for you anyway."

"That's not true!" Said Camille.

"Oh yes it is, he told me. "Your old man was a straight shooter. The day I went in to ask for permission to marry you, he said he didn't have a choice because he knew that you and I were in love. He said I was not strong enough to lead his company. He said he thought you and Archie made a better team. What he didn't know was that I was never interested in running his business. We were going to build our own empire. I will give him credit. I learned a lot under his leadership. His one fault was that he wanted to control the people he loved. That was how he showed his love.

"Anyway, after that day, I got out of Georgia and ended up in Charlotte. I studied and got my real estate license, I have my own agency, with one agent. Also, I sale insurance for State Farm. I'm not MacMillian wealthy, but I'm okay. Now insurance that's where the money is."

"WAIT!" what happened to the lady and the baby?"

"Well, a few days after I had come to tell you, she called and said she wasn't ready to be a mother, that it would interfere with her singing career. She had an abortion. I didn't have any say in that either. I wanted to come back to you, but what would I say?" "He grinned, and your mother would have shot me on sight and rightfully so." They giggled like two middle school kids.

"I see you are still silly. But seriously Jonathan why are you here?"

"Well, mom's health started to go down and I was traveling back and forth, so I decided to get licensed here for real estate and insurance. These day you can easily do business anywhere on the computer. But I hope to start a home health company. I was so thankful for those lady as they helped to take care of mom that I want to put together a nice benefits package for these earthly angels. Like your dad said, "**Take care of your employee, and they will take care of your business.**" Too bad I can never get a chance to tell him how much I admired him."

"I didn't know dad felt that way about you"

"I was okay because he was so frustrated with all of us. Archie was drooling for Chloe, had her head in the clouds, and you and I were like two kids in a candy shop most of the time. Nothing was going his way. I heard that Chloe and Archie recently tied the knot. I knew those two would get together."

"How did you know all this?"

"It's my gift of observation. It's like when your father started up Perfect Image for Chloe. I saw you change, you were not laughing as much anymore. All you wanted to do was work to please your father, and our time together became all about the company," "Have I answered all of your question?"

"Wow, yes you have, and I must admit, I was trying to get Daddy's attention." Said Camille.

"Now it's my turn. What's with this guy Sly?"

"He's a client?"

Jonathan raised an eyebrow. "Remember my gift of observation, you want to try again."

"Business Partner?"

"Okay, a new relationship. I'm really not sure."

"That's okay, I think for now this is where we need to be laughing again as friends.

Camille drove home that night, but she didn't remember how she got there."

"Sly had called while she was in the car. She'll call him back once she was inside the house.

"Hey, honey, I can't talk long. I have a client, but I'll check my scheduled, I can't do it Friday."

"I have too much scheduled that I can't cancel. I've got a shipment coming in and I really want to go there for it. Can't Chloe go with you?"

"She's on her honeymoon, remember."

"Oh, that right, You don't have anyone else you can call?"

"Don't worry, I will make it work. She hung up the phone, That man reminded her of someone."

Camille called Cynthia to ask her to take her on Friday morning. Cynthia said she would be glad to take Camille to the hospital for the procedure, but Terrence also had a doctor appointment too. Camille thanked her for her consideration. So, Camille did the only thing she knew to do.

"Hello Jonathan."

Jonathan helped her into the car. This felt so natural to Camille, but why? This was a man she had not seem in six years just a few days ago. Was she being stupid, why was he even here? He helped her into her condo. After getting her safely into her bed, he said I will be right back.

He went to the car and returned with an overnight bag, and a takeout dinner from Red Lobster... he even had the garlic bread. Sly would not approve "What are you doing?" Fixing breakfast. He set before her a beautiful breakfast, bacon, eggs, grits, toast, and jelly. Should she eat it? Yes!

Just as Jonathan was taking the plates from the table the phone rang.

Hello, Hi Sly, A friend, no don't worry, do what you have to, I'M fine. Bye."

"Sorry"

"For what? It's a conversation that had to happen. Well, I think you can handle it from here."

"I better go. He reached down to give her a hugs. Camille kissed him softly, tenderly, on the lips. He pulled her arms from his neck. "No, I won't let you make the same mistake that I did." He kissed her forehead, picked up his overnight bag and left.

Camille was frustrated, Sly saved her, but for what. Jonathan had saved her but why? It would be nice to talk to her mother about this, but she would never understand back tracking to a bad relationship. She could hear her now "Don't be stupid Camille!" But what was she supposed to do with her heart?

All of these thought and feelings were running around in her head. She did not have a girlfriend to talk to either. Cynthia was a counselor. But a potential business partner. You never show your hand in business so soon. After much consideration, she spoke words that she thought she would never say. **Thank God, Chloe would be home Monday.**

"Hi Cookie"

"Hey girl! "The ladies gave each other a kiss on the cheek.

"This was a great idea, a late lunch after a soothing massage." Said Cynthia.

"Massage?" "So, you are finally enjoying some of your new fount wealth."

"Well not exactly, it was a business meeting."

"Business meeting?" Cookie looked puzzled.

"With Camille MacMillian"

"Oh yeah, I remember. "You two talking business?"

"Yeah, but enough about me...why did you want to see me?

"Well, the show is going well. You know my supervisor that set me up. He brought in one of his friends to hear me. He thought I was really good. This friend has a studio, and he is connected in the music industry."

Cynthia sat back in her chair.

"They believe I could really take off, but I need to go into the studio. People are already asking for CDs after the shows. I would need to hire a band, get some new rags, and backups singers, I figure it would take about 25,000 dollars to set things up right.

25,000.00 dollars, Cynthia said slowly. "Cookie that's a lot of money"

"Studio time isn't cheap. You have to pay techs and bands, background, it expensive."

"Cookie, I don't know if this is a good idea, and I don't know if Bryant will go along with this."

"Bryant?" "What does he have to do with this?" "It's your money! GOSH Cynthia you wouldn't have this money if it weren't for me."

Cynthia was beyond angry.

"Bryant is my husband, and thanks to you, we are in a rough place right now. There is no way I can bring this to him. He would never approve this."

"Did he ask permission when you gave the money to the church, and of course it was his idea to put most of the money in a trust. My GOD, when are you going to grow some BALLS!"

Cynthia snatched open her purse and rifled through to find her checkbook. She could barely write as she tried to press down her angrier.

"I am sick of you always accusing me of being gutless. Well, I had enough guts six years ago when you needed me to go with you for an abortion. Something I never wanted to be a part of, and Bryant still doesn't know about. I have to live with that in our marriage every day. You are always pulling me into your mess. This is the last time. I hope it is worth our friendship." She shoveled the check to Cookie and left.

The cruise had been wonderful Archie and Chloe had spent every minutes of the seven days together. "I will never forget this week." Said Chloe. She buckled her seat buckled up and took Chloe's hand.

"You will never know how much I love you. This has been wonderful. But we must get back to reality."

"Chloe, I was thinking, maybe we should focus on Perfect Image. After all your father did establish it with you in mind."

"Archie stop, daddy only wanted to use my face, because that was all he thought that I had to offer. And up until recently that was all I contributed to it. You and Camille have the expertise to do that, and I don't mind helping but consulting and marketing. I don't, and it requires long working hours. Frankly, I am happy in the background. I really would like to give events a chance, it new, and creative. I think it is my niche."

Chloe took Archie's hand.

"I understand what you are feeling more than you think I do. But having we been talking about long suffering in Bible study? Have faith, everything will work out the way it should, but you must be patient." She turned her head toward the window and closed her eyes.

Archie looked disappointed. He did not want to spend another minute doing busy work for the crumbles tossed to him by Camille. Marketing was challenging. He enjoyed the research, and the power of persuasion, the closing of the deal. If Chloe were not going to help him take the lead of the Perfect Image Consultant Firm; he would have to find another way. But deep down he knew Chloe was right. He hated these new feeling of entitlement, but there was no denying it...they were there.

Chloe walked into Camille's office. "Hi Sis," The sisters embraced. *"I really missed you."* Said Camille.

"How was the cruise?"

"Oh! Camille, it was great. We had such a good time." We took so many pictures, we had to come home to get some rest."

Archie entered, *"Camille, how's everything?"*

"Everything is fine. We actually were able to keep things going in your absence, she smiled. No, I really missed you, both of you." Archie smiled and left the room. Chloe was following behind him when Camille asked Chloe to stay.

She began to share with her everything that had happened while she had been gone. About the doctor and the procedure, how Sly couldn't be there for her. How he was like their father, all about business, about Jonathan and the back story she never knew, how he was so attentive when she had the procedure.

But mostly, she shared with her what her heart really felt and her state of confusion. Chloe smiled, *"believe me I understand you better than you think I do.* She took a big sigh. *"Camille have you ever rode the metro to downtown?"*

"What?" Camille was thinking; What does a bus ride have to do with her problem.

"Well, they have these seat that you can sit in, that are backward to the way in which you are traveling. When you ride backward you can see where you have already been, but then you think what use is that information. "What is important is where you are going?"

"I'm not sure what to tell you. But I know that since I have been going to Bible study; I have this calm, confidence, that I never had before. I've learned that God doesn't want us to live small meaningless lives. He wants us to walk in faith, to step boldly into the sunlight. He certainly doesn't want us to seek man's approval."

"I can't tell you what to do, but before you do anything. Come to revival with me tomorrow night.

Meanwhile, start a conversation with God. Pray with a sincere heart."

Chloe stood up and left Camille to figure out, how to stop riding through life backward?"

Chloe and Archie was waiting for Camille when she arrived. The church revival was sparely attended.

But Camille was glad to be there. She was hoping that she would leave with answers, or at least the courage to do what was right for her life.

She had done what Chloe told her. She started a dialogue with God about Jonathan, and Sly, and her place in the family business and her future happiness.

But mostly, she asked God how not be afraid anymore. She has come to realized that she had lived most of her life afraid. Afraid that she wasn't pretty enough, afraid she wasn't smart enough, afraid she wasn't strong enough, just afraid of disappointing everyone around her.

Reverend Jackson came to the front of the church's pulpit. *"Good Evening, my brothers, and sisters, I thank God for your presence. There are many places you could be, but you chose to be here at revival. Revival is a time to refresh, review, release, and rededicate ourselves to God."*

I hope that most of you were able to attend the Watch Night Service this past New Year's Eve. Because if you were, you heard a brilliant sermon entitled **"A Chance To Begin Again"** *Everyone chuckled. It was such a good sermon, and some of you were probably asleep that night so I have decided it was worth hearing again. Now I didn't have to confess that this was a recycled sermon, but what is revival about? It is about taking what you have, putting away the parts that don't work and sheering up that which does, and moving forth."*

You see each and every day is a chance for every one of us to press the forward button. From Genesis to Revelations, man stumbles and fall, and every time Our Father is there to pick him up, brush him off and gives him the chance to start again.

He never closes the door on us. *You messed up, I don't want any parts of you. You are disobedient...no he doesn't do that! he accepts us just as we are, with all of our shortcomings, our faults. He accepts us unclean, broken, confused, and set us on a path or righteousness. To live boldly in faith, resting in the comfort that he will never leave us or forsake us.*

He did it for the Israelites time and time again. he did it for Abram, he did it for the Job, Joseph and he will do it for you Just as he did for them.

He knows that we won't always get it right, and like a small child we will snatch our hands from his and decide we can do this by ourselves. But know that he is GOD of second chances through his son Jesus Christ we received his grace and mercy. Amen.

Camille awoke the next morning feeling something she had not felt in a very long time, Joy! She took her newly altered black suit from the cleaner bag and put it on her new body. made sure her makeup was neat, yet tasteful for a CEO. her 2" block heels were appropriate for two very important business meetings she had today. but first she needed to send a very important text message.

Camille walked through the front doors of Maximum Impact Spa/Gym. It had been almost a year now. She was thankful that her mother led her here. This was the place where things began to come together to make sense. Last night's revival revealed that God had been with her through it all. He was with her as she began to put together all of the pieces of her fragmented life. Sly entered the conference room; "Hey baby, I only have few minutes. What did you want to see me about?

"Sly have a seat." Camille pulled from her briefcase, data reports. She handed them to Sly. "Sly this is the data that we have collected for New Tricks"

Sly looked puzzled?

"I will not be going forth with this project. I realized this was your dream not mine, and I was just going along to get along, and I'm not doing that anymore."

"WAIT! I thought we had a deal here?" Sly proclaimed calmly.

"Sly, you are a wonderful businessman, and I know you will make "New Tricks" happen. But you live a very surface life. I know because I've done the same thing. We never really get into the game. We stand on the sidelines watching everyone else, cheering them on because we are afraid of failing at life. But I've learned very recently that we are suppose to live life in victory every day. That doesn't we will not make mistakes, but fear cannot be our driver, it must be God the Holy Spirit telling us to step out in FAITH."

"Now I am going to give you some free marketing advice. Cynthia is a very bright young woman. She would be a great resource between you and the community. You should at least talk with her about this project. Plus, she has the means to invest. All good businessmen know you never spend your own money.

"Don't be afraid to give people a chance, you took a chance on me and look how I turned out." Camille stood to leave. she hugged Sly and whispered in his ear."

"Thank you for helping me find my way back; and when you are ready, I will be there for you to begin your journey. And By the way you have an hour free this afternoon. Because I am starting my new membership at LA Fitness, and my new female trainer."

Camille left the gym feeling like she had lost an additional 185 lbs. (Sly). The truth is she knew that Sly and she was not working. Thank God, he had given her the courage to Just Get Out. She wondered why is it that we, especially women are unable to just say this isn't working for me. Thanks to Chloe she had plugged into a new power source, that had freed her, and it was free.

Camille was in her office going through her drawers, she found one of her old friends… an Oreo cookie. She smiled as she sat in her big boss chair. The chair where her father once sat and orchestrated his empire. She had watched him takes his father's small corner grocery store in the black business street, and turned it into a corporation of diversified businesses worthy of its own building in the downtown business district in a major metropolitan city.

She smiled when she thought of his philosophy of surrounding yourself with good people, and they will take care of your business. To think that his own daughter had never felt good enough for him. To this very day he had never said *"Good Job Camille!" "I'm proud of you."* and now he never will. He had reserved that for Chloe, and it was not her fault that he always seemed to encourage her. Yet, she knew he loved her, just differently.

Knock, Knock.

"Come in Chloe, I was just thinking of you. Is Archie on his way?"

"yes, he was on the phone when I left."

"I'm kinda glad he is not here, I wanted to thank you for inviting me to church. I was in the deep end of the ocean and had no idea of how to get back to shore. I also want to ask you for your forgiveness." Chloe looked confused.

"I was so jealous of the way daddy loved you, and that wasn't your fault... Please forgive me for all of the times that I may have said or done that hurt you. I know I never said it back then, but I was proud of you every single time you walked across a stage."

"Chloe laughed, "It is so funny that you say that. I was always praying asking God to make me smart like you. The confidence and respect that dad had for you always made me feel so stupid. I wished

I were you. I guess he loved us both equally, but differently. We were blessed to have a father who was there for us."

"Hi bother in law." Have a seat."

Archie moved to take the seat next to Chloe, when Camille said, "No," she stood up and moved from her big boss desk and walked Archie to his now big boss chair. This is where you belong. I'm stepping down as CEO. This is not my seat, it never was."

Chloe embraced her big sister and said, "You are going to be the best auntie ever."

"AUNTIE!" Camille was happy for her little sister and her brother-in-law.

"Boss, can I have the afternoon off? I have another appointment. Said Camille. "And one more phone call and I will be out of here."

"Hello Cynthia. This I Camille."
"Hi Camille, what's up?"
"I'm fine, and thanks so much for helping me out the other day. I called to tell you I will not be going forth with the "New Tricks" project. I suggested that Sly give you a call, I hope that was alright."
"That's fine I will be looking out for his call."
"What did Bryant say? Is he on board?"
"He fine."
"That's great, I hope we can work together at another time."
"Goodbye"
"Take care."
"Camille had just one more loose end to tie.

Cynthia could not believe the deception that had just come from her mouth. Where had that huge lie come from? Her soul wept. But she reassured herself that if she continued to chill Bryant out, he would agree to anything to get back into her good graces. Besides, she could not stop thinking of all the possibilities that were running through her head; business owner, board of directors, spoke person, council on children's health, all sound better than…school counselor.

As the day progressed Camille was feeling more and more alive. She had been real "Walking Dead." When you live in fear, you are not really living.

But now she could feel a new spirit. She was on her way to IHOP to a date she should have kept six years ago.

Jonathan had asked for her forgiveness and said she still had his heart, but that was so long ago. She was not the same person that she was back then. But she couldn't and wouldn't go back to living a dead life. She was moving forth. She drove into the parking lot. It was as if every parking spot was taken, and the one that wasn't the other drive was too far over. She hated it when people did that. She squeezed her way out of her car door. She nearly tripped as she nervously walked toward the restaurant door.

"Would he be there? She did not see his car. He was rarely late. Maybe he had second thoughts. Suddenly, there he was coming toward her. He opened the door, and she leaped into his arms.

"Let's go get those pancakes." She said.

"Absolutely, but, but before we go in, I see after six years, you still can't park a car." They laughed like no time had ever interrupted their love for one another.

Did she finally have all of the pieces she needed to find her peace.?

Lately, the hustle and bustle of the Jackson household seemed calm and quiet. Cynthia and Bryant were only going through the motions. Their intense conversations about everything had disappeared. They even avoided being in the same room with each other. But the most telling sign was that love had left the bedroom, not the physical act, but the emotional and spiritual kind. Bedtime was a special time for them. Just before going off to sleep, they would reflect on the day's events, and concerns, and then closed with prayer. This had been a sacred time for them. It was sad how easily one night had slipped into two, three, four…and she wondered would they ever find their way back.

Cynthia wondered, if she should accept that she was the cause of these new dynamics…or was she? She could not believe that he had taken revenge on her in the pulpit. She had always supported him in whatever he did, and never complained about his absences from home when he was on one of his community crusades, or nights when he would be in his study for hours, broken *dates and* appointments. While she fermented for years keeping the home fires burning.

Yet, she makes one mistake, and he can't find any of the compassion that he so willingly extends to everyone else. For once couldn't he play the supporting role.

Cynthia knows that Bryant was a great guy, and what woman would not want a husband that seeks a relationship with God before anything else. He is kind, caring and thoughtful.

The qualities that her mother emphasis to encourage their relationship. Her mother had made it clear **that *failure was not an option.*** She made it clear she expected her nest to be empty, and for it to stay that way. So, making the right choices were crucial, and ***your choice of spouse is the most important decision you would ever make.***

Back then Bryant, Cookie and she were the few teenagers that attended and participated in all church activities faithfully. Cookie participated because she had no choice, and she loved to sing. But she and Bryant shared a need to please their parents and God. Bryant was respectful, unlike other girls she had not been pressured into having sex early and getting pregnant. Everyone just accepted that she and Bryant were sat aside, **"the perfect match."** Up until this bump in the road, the water never had been troubled and their lives had been smooth sailing. It had exposed the undercurrent of real emotions and questioned was this real or a fairy tale.

Knock, Knock, "Can I come in?" Asked Cynthia.

"Of course, please come in." Bryant said anxiously.

Cynthia took a seat in front of his desk. "I know you are busy, but I need to run a few things by you."

"Okay, you have my full attention."

"Well, I am not taking Terrence out of Daycare for the summer."

Bryant looked puzzled.

"I thought you were looking forward to the time you would have with him?"

"I will keep him some days, but I have some things I want to explore this summer.

"I am joining the Maximum Impact gym in Grove Park."

"Grove Park, Why so far away? L.A. Fitness is just a few streets over." Said Bryant.

"I want to join Maximum Impact; I want to support this gym."

"Okay, maybe we can do it together?" Said Bryant.

"Don't take this the wrong way, I will purchase you a membership, but I won't schedule my workout around you. The next thing is I'm planning a family vacation. I am taking the family on a cruise. I plan to take my mother. Do you think your mother would like to come too?"

"Okay, I will check my calendar and get some dates to you."

"Bryant, no offense, but you can give me the dates, and I will try to work around them as best as possible. But it will not be the priority, this is last minute, so we may have to take what we can get."

"What happen to school.?" You seemed so sure you wanted to get your Phd where are those plans now?" Bryant looked puzzled.

"I **have options now, something I have never had**" Cynthia got up and left the room.

"Do you need anything before I go to bed."

Bryant shook his head slowly as if he were disappointed. Cynthia closed the door softly. Bryant had no idea who he had just had a conversation with. Certainly, not the soft spoken, lovely woman he fell in love with when he was just a boy and she a girl. They had held each other's hand as they stepped into adulthood. All he knew was he really missed her.

He knew and accepted that the money was the elephant in the room crowding out their relationship. Certainly, money is a blessing, and because of her generosity the church did not have to be concerned about the HAVC. Yet in the same vein it had made she and Cynthia examine their relationship.

Both he and Cynthia were guilty of being too accommodating. As teenagers they willingly did whatever was asked of them, while their counterparts gave way to youthful frolicking. He recalled his father pointing her out as a godly woman, as the kind of woman that would make an excellent pastor's wife." *"The wife of a pastor is as important as the pastor himself, not every woman can be a pastor's wife*, his father would say. But Cynthia had been easy to love. She was kind, polite, and respectful, unlike other girls, even his own sister.

Both he and Cynthia were held to a higher standard, set aside for God's work. They had found refuge in each other as they traveled the road to their current destination as pastor and first lady.

Cynthia had been a virgin when they married and so had he; their love had been *pure* in every sense of the word.

He prayed that she and he would keep their hands in God's hand and not grasp after the ways to the world. He asked God for guidance for their union.

Michael was Cookie's biggest fan. He was seated front and center every Friday evening sometimes for both sets. Out of respect she would visit his table to thank him for his support. But she was careful not to stay to long, as not to give him the wrong impression.

So why was there a woman seated at his table tonight. She could not tell who she was, but of all the night spots in the city; why would he bring her here? They were having drinks and making small talk. She was shaken but the show must go on.

Cookie retreated to her makeshift dressing room in the storage room of the lounge. There among the bar's inventory, she wondered if he would still be there at her second set? Why did he bring her here... *especially tonight.*

"Hello"
"Is this Cynthia Jackson?"
"Yes, it is."
This is Sly we met at the wedding Camille's friend, she suggested that we talk."
"Yes, she mentioned that you might call."
"When can you come to the gym?"
"How does this afternoon around 4 o'clock?"
That will be fine, I will be here. I'll see you then."

As Cynthia hung up, she wondered should she tell Bryant now or wait until she had talked to Sly. There may be nothing to tell. Still, she felt she was sneaking behind Bryant's back...maybe because she was.

Maximum Impact's conference room

Cynthia sat in the conference room and waited for Sly's arrival. She knew nothing about the world of business and even less than anything about a gym. Yet here she sat about to have her first grown up business meeting she had ever had all by herself.

Camille had not told her very much about Sly except that he was somewhat of a male chauvinist but weren't most men. Even in a female dominated profession like education; male educator often think they should be in leadership positions, so that character flaw she could handle. The fact that she found him physically attractive, well that was new ground too. She had never really given much attention to other men.

Sly entered the room pleasant enough. He was carrying the "New Tricks" file from Perfect Image Agency. He shook Her hand and began talking.

"*Camille tells me you may be interested in expanding your horizons. I don't know how much she has told you, so I thought I would give you the information and let you look over it and give me a call." He stood, shook her hand, and left.*

"Okay," Cynthia said to herself. She just wasn't sure what had happened. This man thinks he can work with children?" He's not a chauvinist, he's crazy.

Cynthia gathered up the file and her pocketbook, and headed for her car, next thing she knew she was standing directly in front of Towanda.

"Towanda, what are you doing here?"

"*I work nearby, I think I should be asking you the same question, you are little far out of the neighborhood.*"

"*I'm here because I'm thinking about joining.*" Said Cynthia.

"*What is that in your hand?*" Asked Towanda.

"*Oh nothing,*" said Cynthia.

Towanda smiled slyly. "*Don't worry, what happens at Maximum stays at Maximum. But I am glad to see you because I didn't know how to come back and apologized for the way I acted in your office that day. I was having a bad day and took it out on you. But Girl, you don't know how hard it is to be a single woman in this world, and I pray you never do.*"

"*Don't give it another thought I'm a counselor, I'm use to being yelled at by angry parents. How is Mariah doing, what is she doing this summer?*"

"*Mariah is going through something…I don't know how to help her. I just hope she will come through it okay. This summer she is taking Drivers Ed and math camp. I don't like her spending so much time alone but she's too old for a babysitter.*"

"*Well. I'm keeping her in my prayers, at least she and Jennifer are mending. Towanda, I really need to go…I need to pick up Terrence.*"

"*Oh, before you go guess who I ran into the other night at the Westmont Lounge?*"

"*Who?*"

"*Michael, from church, he is really a nice guy. He kinda rescue me. I got stood up. My dinner date never showed. Girl it is rough out here trying to find a good man. Tell me, do you know if he is seeing anyone?*"

"*I'm not sure. How was the entertainment? Asked Cynthia slowly.*

"*Cookie? Towanda shrugged her shoulders. "She was good.:*

"*Towanda, I'm sorry but I've got to get my son, take care, and tell Mariah I said, "Be Good."*"

"*Okay, see you.*" Said Towanda.

Driving home Cynthia now had someone to measure Bryant against. *How about Sly?* She could think of a few things she would call him, and chauvinist wasn't one of them. Bryant would have never entered a room the way he did. If he thinks he has what it takes to work with kids and parents, then he has a rude awakening coming. But she still believed in the project, or maybe she was stepping out too big too soon. Just then her phone rang... It was Cookie, what did she want? Cynthia wasn't sure she was ready to talk with her... but she might be hurt or sick.

"Hello."

"Hey Cynthia."

"Cookie" Cynthia could hear the sadness in her voice. *"Is everything alright?"*

"Cynthia, I really need to talk to you... in person."

"Cookie, I am on my way to get Terrence, couldn't you just tell me on the phone?"

Cynthia could hear her sniffling of emotion coming from Cookie's phone. Okay, I will call you back in 10 minutes.

Cynthia called Jennifer to see if she could get Terrence for her and found she had already picked her little brother up from daycare.

"What a daughter!"

Cynthia called Cookie back and wondered what her story was this time. Why couldn't she cut this girl from her life? Maybe sisters of love can be as close as sisters of blood.

Cynthia agreed to meet Cookie at Apple Bee's, she didn't know what Cookie she would meet up with; but one thing for sure she was not going to be hit up for more money. She had not even told Bryant about the $25,000 and this time she would not be caught off guard. She intended to give her a gift anyway, but Bryant insisted that we move slowly incorporating the money into their lives.

They met in the lobby, and greet each other with a hug and kiss on the cheek. For Cynthia today the greeting seemed fake. But she was willing to listen.

"Thank you so much for coming Cynthia. I couldn't blame you if you refused to see me. After the way I behaved the last time, we met. First, I want to thank you for always being there for me no matter what the situation is, and boy have I put you in some situations. The nerve of me referring to you as **gutless**. You have more heart and strength then anyone I know, and if you decide to cut me out of your life, I understand. I want to tell you...you and Bryant were right; I need to grow up."

"Well, I am glad you are getting your head on straight. It isn't that we... I don't believe in you, we. I just wanted you to be aware that life is serious." Said Cynthia

"Yes, Life is serious, and boy did I find out the hard way."

"What are you talking about? Asked Cynthia.
"The MONEY! The money is all gone?" Cookie's eyes filled with tears.
"GONE! What do you mean GONE?
"Mr. Reagan, and his friend, I met with them after you gave me the money. I gave the money to him to set things up... Well, I didn't hear from him. He wouldn't return my calls. So, I talked to Mr. Reagan, and he pretty much told me to get out of his face...that he had nothing to do with it and that was that. I feel so stupid, why do I always do stupid things? Nothing good ever comes my way. Bryant is right I am a disgrace to the family."
"Cookie, Bryant never said you were a disgrace or stupid... He loves you. Love is not always neat and pretty. Sometimes love is tough and truthful. Sometimes confrontational. Bryant is just afraid you might get hurt or be taken advantage of like this situation. Stop being so hard on yourself you did nothing wrong. Mr. Reagan and his friend are just shady. Don't you worry, Bryant will know what to do."

Cynthia was all set to defend her position about going into the gym business, but, once again it is all about Cookie. she had not told him about the money. Now she had to tell him she had once again gone behind his back; plus tell him the real reason she was joining the gym, and she expected him to help Cookie get the money back. Because he is the only hero, they both have.

Cynthia arrived home to find that Bryant and Terrence were not at home but, Jennifer was home. She wondered if Jennifer had noticed the change in her and Bryant's relationship. She knew this could affect her, if she felt her home life was in jeopardy. She yelled upstairs and asked her to come downstairs
"Jennifer, can you come down here please?"
"Yeah, mom."
"Where is your father and Terrence?"
"They went to get something to eat, I made myself something here."
"I am sorry I wasn't here to fix dinner, but hopefully things will be getting back to normal. Jennifer, where are you and Mariah with your relationship now that school is out?"
"We talk...but things are not the same. When I am with her, I can't get that day out of my mind. I don't hate her; I don't feel safe around her. So, for now I will love her from a distance."
"You know it sounds like you two are on track. It takes time to rebuild trust once a relationship has been bruised. It's like an open wound, it has to be cared for while it heals. I think you two will heal, but it may leave a scar.

In this case and where you are in life, this scar could be a good thing as you go out in the world and start new relationships."

I am planning a cruise, and I was wondering would you like to invite her?"

"Let me think about it, what about Keisha?"

"Of course, she can come too."

Just then the door opened, and Terrence and Bryant were coming in from dinner.

"Jennifer, will you take Terrence upstairs and watch him for me?"

"Sure, Come on Terrence, let's go to my room."

"Well, how was the gym?"

"It was ok, it wasn't quite as exciting as I thought would be so, That's up in the air. Can I talk to you about a couple of things?"

"Sure."

"First, let me start off by saying I know I have been acting a little crazy these last few weeks. I think the old folks use to say, **"I've been smelling myself."** *They both smiled. "but the idea of OPTIONS!*

Open up a world of possibilities that I have never considered before. Did you ever think that you and I didn't have an option? We just sort of did what was expected of us. Like did you always want to be a pastor?"

Did you at least look at another woman? I guess these thoughts had been pushed to the back of my mind, but now...now my mind won't stop thinking of the possibilities."

Cynthia, I always knew I had options. Serving God is my privilege, loving you is the same. I felt the calling of the Lord from the crib. He placed you in my life. He said he would supply my every need...he knew I needed you. And you have been a blessing to my life." He took her hand.

"This is just a test that we must go through, and in the end, we will be stronger for it. All I can tell you is you must pray and ask God for guidance. You need to call on the Holy Spirit to give you your PEACE."

"Thank you." Cynthia said softly. She then took the folder she had received from Sly and placed it in Bryant's hand.

"This is a folder of an idea. Will you look at it with an open mind and tell me what you think?"

"Of course, I will."

"I'm not finish." Cynthia took a deep breath..."I gave Cookie $25,000.00."

Bryant raised his eyebrows, and said, *"That was nice of you."*

"No, it wasn't, *I did it in angrier. She egged me on, and I wrote her the check and threw it at her. I am so ashamed.*

Bryant looked surprised. *"That's not like you. What happened?*

*"Cookie does not understand a marriage relationship, but that's not the point. She has been taken advantage of and all of her money was taken by this man, and **she feels just awful.**"*

Bryant took a deep breath and asked for the details.

Westmont Hotel

Bryant arrived at the Westmont Hotel along with Michael. He walked up to the front desk and asked to speak to Mr. Reagan.

Bryant noticed that Michael seemed a little anxious.

"Michael, we are here to talk, you are my witness. We are agents of God. Just keep those thoughts in mind." Suddenly, Mr. Reagan walked over and invited them to his office.

"Have a seat gentlemen, how can I help you?" Bryant and Michael took a seat.

"Mr. Reagan, This is Mr. Johnson, he is a Deacon at the church where I am the pastor."

Gentlemen, if you are here to solicit a donation; that is done through the corporate office. I can give you the address." said Mr. Reagan.

"I only wish it were that simple. My sister sings in the lounge and you introduced her to a crook."

Mr. Reagan sat back in his chair. "Who stole 25,000.00 dollar from her." I would like her money back in full by Thursday night before she performs her first set." Said Bryant.

"Rev. Jackson, I had nothing to do with that. I'm sorry Cookie lost her money, but there is nothing I can do."

"I am sorry too, Mr. Reagan, How long have you been with this company? I imagine you probably have a pretty good retirement plan and benefit package."

Bryant paused. "I'll take that corporation address and phone number now."

Mr. Reagan stood up. And so did Michael. he extended his hand to Bryant.

"Rev. Jackson that will not be necessary."

Bryant stood and shook his hand and said "Mr. Reagan, thank you for your time, and always walk in truth. Good day to you.

Michael and Bryant were laughing on their way home.

"He thought I was your enforcer." Said Michael.

"I don't care what he thought, all I know that come Thursday, he and his little friend better have Cookie's money in her hand."

"Do you want me to oversee the transaction?" *You know it is no problem, I have been here Thursday night since she started. Michael said.*

"No, I am sure Mr. Reagan got God's will loud and clear, and his will be done."

Michael nodded in agreement.

"What do you mean you have been here every Thursday since she started?" Bryant wasn't sure that was good for either Michael or Cookie. It is not good to live in the past. They were not the teenage lovers of 20 years ago. They both had acquired some baggage, some filled with dirty laundry.

"Cookie is really a sweetheart. She is just trying to find her way. I'm praying for."

Bryant shook his head, "LOVE, really is Longsuffering."

Cynthia called to see how Cookie was doing.
"Hi Cookie, How are feeling today?"
"Hi, I'm okay."
"Well, I confessed everything to your brother. I think we are on the road to recovery."
"EVERYTHING?" How did he take it?
He was very concerned for you, you know he loves you, you're his baby sister.
What did he say?... **I told you so.** Cookie said in despair.
"No, actually he was very supportive, and sorry that you had been taken advantage of by Mr. Reagan and his friend. I think he and Michael were going over to see him today, to try and get some understanding of the situation.
"What good is that going to do?"
"Darling, your brother speaks with the high authority of our Lord Jesus. Where is your faith."
"Did you said Michael too, why would he go?"
"You tell me, I hear he had a guess the other night."
"How did you hear about that?"
"A little bird told me that he rescued her from being stood up, and that little bird wanted to know if he was seeing anyone special?"
"And I will not be surprised, if that little bird starts back to be attending church regularly, instead of just sending her daughter."
"Little bird my foot, sounds more like a hawk! But I can't blame her, he would be a nice bird to nest with. Said Cookie.

Thursday Night/Lounge Night

"Ladies and gentlemen, you have been so wonderful this night and every night since I started here. But sadly, this engagement has come to an end. I want to take this time to thank Mr. Reagan for all of his encouragement, and this lovely band for their beautiful support. I really could not have had this experience without you.

You know family is so important. Family doesn't kick you when you are down instead; they become the wind beneath your wings."

She looked up, and her eyes teared up.

"I'm blessed to have such a family. I thank God for my wonderful brother and my sister of the heart. They are my guiding light, and I am sure if you asked them, they would say it has not been easy. Thank you for lighting my path when I lose my way. Also thank you Lord for a very good friend that made sure each week I got off to a good start.

As some of you know I always close with "You're nobody, until somebody loves you... but tonight, I've got a new song to sing... **Amazing Grace, how sweet the sound....**

SUNDAY MORNING/NEW JERUSALEM BAPTIST CHURCH

Cynthia looked across the congregation of the church. This Sunday morning's service was the same, yet different. There were so many familiar and not so familiar faces in the crowd. Camille and Jonathan had come to the same place and sat next to Chloe and Archie. Cookie had managed to make it to service on time, and Michael couldn't be happier to have her seated next to him... And the choir seemed complete with Divine, back in place, standing directly behind Jennifer. Rev. Jackson stood and announced his sermon topic.

(It's A Family Affair)

"Good morning my Brothers and Sisters of New Jerusalem Baptist Church. This morning that greeting takes on a special meaning. Recently, I had an opportunity to sit down and enjoy watching a nature program on the PBS channel. Believe it or not, this is one of my pleasure activities. I enjoy these programs as much as some people enjoy watching a football game. Because *these programs are a testament to the* **Greatness of God**. *This particular program was entitled "LEAVE IT TO BEAVER."*

"Back in the late fifty's there was a television program that was named the same. It was about this middle-class family where the youngest son was nicknamed "Beaver."

"He would innocently make mistakes and require the support of the family to get back on track. But he would especially need his father's guidance to get back on the right foot. Unlike this old television program, this nature program was about a real beaver."

"A beaver is a large rat, (rodent) but unlike some of his cousins. He is not a nuisance. If anyone ever compare you to beaver say...Thank you."

"If ever there was a creature that lives out God's purpose for his life...it is this little animal. The first thing that he does right is that; he goes out and **"seeks"** a mate. They spend a little time together. Once they are in agreement, they then **"mate" for life.**

Next, they start a "homestead." They started off with nothing, but together they keep adding on until they create a "community" where all sorts of animals," in that community. big and small can live together and prosper." And he **"keeps order"** in that community.

Then he and his mate have children. The father lovingly watches over his mate, until the kittens are born. Both the mother and the father teach the children the lessons they will need to go out into the world and start **"a new generation."** This creature is driven by nature to perform God's plan his life.

If only man could be like the beaver... God had a plan for man's life, but from the very beginning man made it... **"A FAMILY AFFAIR."**

The difference in the beaver, and the human creature is that we were made in God's own image, and he granted us the gift of choice. The choice to love him and to seek a relationship with him.

Adam and Eve were offered a deal of a lifetime; but unfortunately, they were disobedient to God's instructions. They allowed Satan to drive a wedge between man and God, and that began man's downward spiral and the destruction of the family. Then along came the children, Cain and Abel, man struggled with sin and deception which brought jealousy and murder. All through the Bible, man has struggled to live out God's purpose for his life.

Joseph's brothers sold him into slavery...sibling rivalry. Rebekkah favored one child over the other...deceived her husband the most sacrifice relationship bringing about abuse, birth right stolen and a child estranged from the family.

And it goes on and on Adultery, adoption, worshiping false Gods, wars, slavery stealing...you name it, and the family members have done it to each other.

I'm sure that all of you has experienced some type of family conflict that you though you would have never had to endure, maybe you are the one causing the conflict; I don't know.

But if you have, my prayer is that you and your family member or members are able to resolve your conflict and move toward **God's purpose for your life.**

Satan has continued his attack on the family, to try to drive a wedge between man and God.

Because God **"loves"** *the family; it is his first and sacred institution. Although, man sinned and continues to sin against him, he always provides "a path back to him" which serves as an example for each of us. We should demonstrate that same kind of love for each other.*

For it is every man, woman, and child's purpose to serve God in all of his glory... to be a part of his kingdom... **his family.**

Yes, my brothers and sisters **"IT's A Family Affair."**

After the service, members met in the atrium of the church, to meet and greet each other. Cynthia went to Bryant's office with Terrence. When Bryant came in, she kissed him on the cheek and said, *"Thank you for choosing to love me."*

Just then came a tap on the door and in walked Cookie with Michael.

"Great sermon Pastor." Cookie hugged him around the waist and Bryant slowly wrapped his arms around his little sister. *"Welcome Home."*

Cynthia's phone began to ring, she stepped to the side of the room to answer.

"Hello, hi Towanda."

"What do you mean **Gone?***"*

Milton Keynes UK
Ingram Content Group UK Ltd.
UKHW031150251124
451529UK00001B/161